"There's no way I could do it again."

Lynn grinned as Kevin's lips nuzzled her neck. She looked into his laughing eyes and continued somewhat breathlessly, "You're wasting your time. I'm completely sated."

"Just lie back and don't worry about a thing," he purred. "I only want to examine your body—for scientific purposes, of course."

She giggled as he began to explore her velvet softness. But by the time he had slowly savored every inch, she was groaning with delight.

"There is one final stage of the investigation," he said at last, his voice husky and deep and suddenly serious.

Lynn's heart was pounding, her face flushed. "What's that?" she whispered urgently.

"Let me show you...."

THE AUTHOR

Born in Texas, Lass Small says she's almost
become a native of her adopted Indiana
through osmosis. Of course, her greatest
love is writing but she also enjoys drawing,
swimming and "visiting." She draws
heavily on her own experiences in her
often humorous work.

This talented author was twice honored
when her first publication received a
Waldenbook Award and was then taped
by the Los Angeles Braille Institute for
the blind and disabled. It is one of
her proudest achievements. Although
Collaboration is her first Harlequin
Temptation, Lass has written several other
books under the pseudonym Cally Hughes.

Collaboration

LASS SMALL

Harlequin Books

TORONTO • NEW YORK • LONDON
AMSTERDAM • PARIS • SYDNEY • HAMBURG
STOCKHOLM • ATHENS • TOKYO • MILAN

To Jan, Robin and Joi
To LaVyrle and Bertrice
To Elaine, Sara, Charlotte
and Janet...
To *all* the marvelous writers
whose imaginations charm
the rest of us.
With my love.

Published April 1985

ISBN 0-373-25154-8

Printed in Canada

LYNN POTTER'S RESTLESS FINGERS worried her short crop of black curls, and she decided she'd listened to her agent long enough. He was calling from New York City. She sighed impatiently into the phone and interrupted his monologue. "Ed—"

But Ed Fulton broke in smoothly and coaxed, "I know you'll work well together."

For the third time Lynn proclaimed stridently, "I work alone!"

"Now, Lynn, give it a try. See him. As it is, his books sell only to diehard science-fiction readers, while yours sell to romantics. Together you'd both command a wider readership. You'd make a stunning combination! He can't write romance and you can't write science fiction, but together you'd—"

"I don't want to write science fiction!" Lynn snapped.

"But it sells so well," Ed wheedled. "He lives in Anderson, not very far from Fort Wayne, out there in Indiana, and—"

"Ed, Anderson is eighty-four miles south of Fort Wayne."

"He could commute for the parts where you combine material. You could write enough of a string to carry through the book. You know, touches and glances and that kind of junk."

" 'Junk'?" she questioned sharply.

"Well...." He began to explain his current attitude toward romance.

"You and Ann are quarreling again," Lynn guessed. "Call her for lunch, ply her with wine and take her to a hotel."

"See? That's what Kevin needs in his book."

" 'Kevin'?" she asked, sounding as if she'd taken a bite of sauerkraut when she'd been expecting sugared strawberries.

"Kevin Walker," Ed responded. "He's a nice lad."

"How much of a lad?" She was becoming hostile. "I haven't the time to baby-sit."

"I believe he's in his late twenties."

"How late?" she asked suspiciously.

Silence.

"Edgar!"

"You called me 'Edgar.' You're as bad as Ann."

"She called you 'Edgar'?" Hostilities were forgotten as Lynn's interest was piqued.

"Geese! Women!" Ed was a little dramatic.

"Yeah, and I'm one of them."

"Aw, Lynn, forgive me." He held out a verbal olive branch. "I feel rotten over this quarrel with Ann. If you'll just forget about Kevin's being a man, you'll realize this could be a very good career move for you."

She ignored him and advised, "Call Ann and have lunch with her in some dim, clandestine hole in the wall."

"You're the expert," he conceded. Then craftily he added the rider. "Will you see Kevin?"

"Will you take Ann to lunch?" she bargained.

"It's a deal!"

"You'd planned to take her, anyway."

"Lynn, you and I have known each other four and a half years, and in reading all those romances, I've picked up a thing or two. I'm not stupid, you know." His chuckle bubbled in her ear. "Milton gave me the key to his suite at the Plaza. I might not be in the office tomorrow, if you should need to get in touch. Oh, and by the way, Kevin will be by later today." And he hung up.

Knowing she'd been manipulated, Lynn looked sourly at the buzzing phone before replacing the receiver. She would be forced to cope with a first encounter. She would have to meet this Kevin person. Damn.

She would make it perfectly clear, crystal clear, to Kevin...Kevin. She stretched the name until it was suitably distorted. It sounded like muscles, piles of muscles, topped by a very small, empty head.

No, that was wrong. Kevin was a writer of science fiction, which meant he was probably scrawny—all arms and legs and Adam's apple, with a great dome-shaped head.

How dare Edgar saddle her with some domehead who lived in a fantasy world? They probably wouldn't be able to communicate at all. He'd just sit there like a lump and blush if she suggested that the characters hold hands.

Lynn restlessly paced her attic apartment, glaring

around until she found something else on which to
focus her attention. There were far too many plants.
She'd had some of them since her first apartment.
She was a junior at Indiana University then, but
she'd quit school to support Steve after they were
married.

Occasionally even Lynn thought it was odd that
she of all people could write tender, loving romances.
With the divorce, ten years ago, had come the knowledge that Steve had used her. She'd worked his way
through college; she'd been cook and bedmate, and
she'd been had. No wonder she'd become...cautious.

Then, two years ago, when she was finally willing
to take another chance with a man and a commitment, Mark Blackwood had cemented her bitter
disenchantment. The first time she'd let down her
defenses in all those years and she'd had to pick
Mark. When he jilted her to marry a predatory
blonde Lynn vowed never again to be caught in
another emotional tangle. It hurt. She'd been burned
twice and knew only a fool would ask for more.

Her life was now exactly as she wanted it. She was
aloof. She did what she wanted, when she wanted
and how she wanted. And she had her writing. She
went and ran her finger over the spines of the growing number of her books that marched along the
privileged shelf.

But now Edgar had boxed her in so that she was
going to have to take emotional energy that she'd
rather invest in her work, in order to tactfully
handle the task of letting a sci-fi writer down gently.
She didn't want to have to deal with a fragile male

psyche, but neither did she want to feel responsible for the destruction of an ego.

She would be careful for Kevin's sake. She knew how terrible it was to be rejected, and she would be kind but firm. She would encourage him in his writing. She could do that. She could tell him how to look at women, how to describe them and how to put his own feelings into his characters' reactions to women. She saw herself in the role of mentor. It could give her an added interest. Her life really was rather . . . lonely.

She might read his manuscripts and guide him into writing smashing best-sellers that would be made into major motion pictures. Then, perhaps, when he was older and could handle it, she'd have an affair with him.

Older women did have affairs, and being over thirty she was an older woman. So an affair would be acceptable. Only an involvement would be unthinkable.

Wait! What if Kevin was like her younger brother's friend Hog. After thirteen years of adolescence he was only now beginning to evolve into something akin to a human being.

Imagine seducing Hog! If he were the last man on earth and the future of humankind were up to them, it would be, "Goodbye, humankind. You take North America, Hog. I'll swim to Europe." Kevin was probably another Hog.

But there was no sense in dwelling on life's cruel jokes. She took her jogging suit from a peg behind the back door and went into her bedroom to put it on. Ready for a brisk, mind-clearing jog, she left the apartment and started down the open back steps. The stairway was more like a fire escape tacked on to the building to conform to fire-safety regulations.

The bitter January wind hit her with such force that she ran back inside to get an undershirt. On her way once again, she pulled a knit cap over her short hair and grabbed gloves and a scarf. Back outside she hesitated, testing the wind and scanning the area.

It was an old neighborhood by the St. Mary's River, north of Foster Park. The trees stood silently frozen, the bushes huddled in scratchy clumps, the grass was a dead brown and the swirling clouds were low and gloomy. There wasn't any snow left from Christmas, but there were dirty patches of ice in treacherous streaks on the deserted streets. It had been a mean winter.

Taking care not to fall on the open steps, Lynn navigated the two flights and set off down the street to Foster Park. The *Writer's Digest* had once scolded authors to get out of their chairs and exercise, and she took all their advice seriously.

As Lynn jogged along, her thoughts turned back to Kevin. She had no real objection to science fiction if it wasn't too technical. Being a romantic, she did enjoy fantasy and magic, larger-than-life heroes and ebony-haired maidens.

She hadn't used long-haired blondes as heroines since Mark eloped with Karen. In order to be as different from Karen as possible, Lynn had cut off her own long, dark hair. Fortunately, all that had been two years ago and she was now over Mark completely.

Two years of consciously avoiding thoughts of Mark, but then dreaming of him, seeing him make love to that woman. Karen had taken one look at Mark and decided she wanted him, and she'd got him. But Mark had been a more-than-willing victim. Men!

"Hey!" a jogging acquaintance yelled. They rarely spoke but paced companionably whenever they happened to meet. Lynn slowed down, her breath ragged, and she knew she'd been going much too fast, trying to outrun her thoughts. She stopped and ran in place as he caught up with her.

He was older, a plodding, methodic man, married with a number of children. Not speaking, she turned, and they continued together, jogging at a much slower rate and stopping at the designated exercise points. Finishing the course, they lifted silent hands to each other and parted.

Walking it off, cooling down, Lynn paused at Mrs. Hobbs's house. The old lady was almost completely bedridden. Lynn whistled under her window, waited until she saw the drape waggle, then went on home. Lynn was one of the neighborhood watchers who kept tabs on housebound people.

Back in her apartment, she showered, then settled down to work for two hours until noon. She was well into writing a quarrel when her alarm clock announced lunchtime. She ate mechanically, oblivious to the bleak, wintry view from her small kitchen table. She used a pad and pencil by her plate as she continued making notations for her book. The lunch dishes joined those from breakfast in the sink before Lynn hurried back to her word processor.

She was so engrossed in trying to keep the spat from getting nasty that she didn't really hear the doorbell at first. She was in the habit of inserting a piece of paper into the bell so it emitted only a muted hum. She raised her head and listened as it repeated. There was no release for the street door from her apartment and the front window was stuck, so she couldn't call down to find out who was there. It would mean running two flights of stairs to find out, and disgruntled, she decided to ignore the buzz.

She had turned back to her keyboard and was successfully resisting her curiosity about who was leaning so persistently on her bell, when she remembered Kevin. No doubt he was out there on her doorstep so immersed in his fantasy world that he wasn't even aware he was freezing to death. He wouldn't have the sense to realize she wasn't going to answer the damned doorbell. He'd simply stand there and turn into ice. And it would certainly be a nuisance to walk around him all winter until spring thaw.

With great ill grace she heaved her body up from her chair. Pulling down her faded purple sweat shirt to meet the top of her jeans, she clomped down the steps, deliberately making noise.

The staircase was a spiral from the third floor down to the second, enclosed in a tower whose space had once been a complete waste. The connecting door to the main house had been walled off, so the entire stairwell was hers alone.

Several years before, Lynn had thrown a party after a Fine Arts Ball and she'd turned her guests loose on the bare walls. They'd drawn a fantastic array of people climbing the steps and created a unique mural. Though the drawings were a little strange, Lynn prized them as she did the friendship of the artists.

Since the landlord saw no reason to heat the stairwell, there being no waterpipes to freeze, Lynn was shivering by the time she peeked out the door. There was a man standing there with his back to her. Bareheaded in spite of the weather, his thick dark hair was ruffled by the wind. He was tall with nice broad shoulders.

At the sound of the door opening he turned toward her. His face was strongly masculine, even though the straight bars of his eyebrows rested above an awful lot of eyelashes. He had a straight nose and a delicious mouth with a full, sensuous lower lip. Lynn was startled by the feeling of sexual attraction that stirred in her body.

As her eyes rested on his square chin she bet he got his way most of the time, and the stirring became a thrill of sensual awareness that caused her to shiver with more than the cold. The impact of his masculinity was so stunning that she stiffened and thinned her lips in self-preservation. "Yes?" she said coolly.

With some wonder in his voice he stated, "You're Lynn Potter." This woman was quite simply stunning. She was about as tall as his nose and filled out even an old sweat shirt and jeans beautifully. Her dark hair was short and attractively tumbled. And a man could lose himself in those sherry eyes.

Ed and Ann had sent him here because they were concerned about this woman. They'd told him she was too withdrawn and that a collaboration with him might just stir her up a bit. "Stir her up"? What about him? He blinked. "Did Ed call? I'm—"

"You're Kevin Walker?" She realized that her surprise was obvious. And into her mind wiggled the thought that she probably wouldn't have to teach this man how to look at a woman. She shook her head in disbelief. There was no way this devastating man could be the scrawny science-fiction writer she'd imagined.

He grinned, causing a new wave of sensation to slide up her spine. "So Ed did call. He and Ann were having one of their quarrels and I wasn't sure if he'd remember." His voice was deep and laced with humor.

If he really is Kevin Walker, she cautioned herself, *this could very easily get complicated. You'd better be careful, Lynn.* Aloud she said only, "Kevin," and stared up at him.

He was charmed. She was so pretty, so feminine, and his mouth quirked as he prompted, "May I come in?"

She automatically stepped back, oddly reluctant, wary and still staring. Why should she feel that allowing him through the door was a dangerous thing to do? How silly.

Kevin moved inside, closed the door and finally had to take her arm in order to encourage her to go up the stairs. She felt adrift in a strange kind of vacuum, while the arm that he held tingled with excitement.

He commented on and stopped to examine some of the characters on the walls. "Why are there feathers pasted on this one?" He touched the three feathers she'd added to one figure for the sake of modesty.

She mumbled something unintelligible. How strange, she thought. Her tongue was tangled.

His response was a rumbling laugh that reverberated inside her as they continued up the spiral and stepped from the stairwell into her apartment. She looked at it with a stranger's eyes and she liked it. The walls were French vanilla and the bare wood floors were scattered with vibrant, hand-loomed rugs. Of course the sofa was a nuisance; it was much too soft. But the plain brown color was good, and it made a handy nest for the needlepoint pillows Lynn's mother turned out with alarming rapidity. And Lynn did realize the apartment wasn't exactly tidy.

But Kevin exclaimed in pleasure, as everyone did, "This is great! Even a fireplace!"

"It was a battle to get it." Her vocal chords decided to run wild. "I had to pay for it myself and get extra insurance on the house, but it's worth it. It's even worth dragging the logs up fourteen flights of stairs."

"Fourteen flights, huh." He appreciated her exaggeration.

"Carrying logs, it's definitely fourteen flights."

"I'll help with the carrying," he promised as he poked around. Her living room took up most of the attic, and the ceiling followed the peaks and slopes of the roofline. The bedroom was a tiny bed-size corner and the rest of the space was divided into a miniature kitchen, a bathroom and some large closets.

Lynn hadn't changed anything in two years. Not since her family had instigated a complete redecoration to help her make a fresh start after Mark. Her brother and sisters had insisted on cheerful, bright colors and Lynn, listless and uninterested, had given them free rein. Now the apartment was really a very pleasant eye-catching place.

With so many friends who were artists, inevitably there were pictures. She'd bought only those she could live with, but the walls were still full. She rarely actually looked at them, but saw them as patterns in negative space.

Kevin took off his coat and went over to hang it on the hall tree. She examined him covertly. Cluttering up an obviously exceptional body was a gray sweater over a tieless dress shirt and gray corduroy trousers. He looked around and then back at her, repeating, "Very nice. I like it."

Unaccountably pleased, she replied inanely, "I plan to get rid of most of the plants this spring when the weather's nicer. Then I can give them away without freezing them."

He appeared to understand that plants needed consideration and that she wasn't simply weird. He asked, "May I sit down?"

She gestured in a preoccupied wave. She was oddly uncertain about what to do next or how to deal with the puzzling squiggle of alarm she felt. His effect on her was quite unsettling.

He finally sat down, leaving her standing, and indicated the package he'd brought along. "Ed told you about the book?"

She nodded, knowing now was the time to set this straight. "I work alone."

"Me, too."

He didn't want to work with her? "It's not that I don't like fantasy...." Her tongue had decided on its own comment.

"Well, I must say I like romance." He grinned, and Lynn experienced the sensation of being licked on the inside of her stomach by a large, lazy tongue.

"What sort of romance do you write?" he asked, giving every appearance of being interested.

"For women," she replied.

"Which one would you recommend I read?" He took a notepad and pencil from his pocket.

"Well—" she moved over to the bookcase "—I do have an extra copy of *Life's Desire* you could borrow." She felt awkward, so her sentences became choppy. "If you want to read one, I like this one. I think it's very good. I shouldn't have said that. Now if you think it's awful you'll feel compelled to think of something kind to say. But—" she paused and added honestly "—I do like it and I think it's more typical of...well, it's not the usual run...." Her voice trailed off as she realized how Kevin was looking at her.

"I see," he said, still looking. His body was alert in an exciting way. He wasn't threatening. It was just that he was so alive, so vital.

When the silence stretched on too long Lynn asked, "You know Ed and Ann, then?"

"I went out and spent a week with them on the coast. They're—" he groped for the right word "—interesting."

"They are totally out of touch with the real world." Lynn supplied her evaluation, then added, "He's a superb agent, though."

"This is my tenth book, but it's the first time I've had an agent. He thinks I could do better with some romance in my writing. I'm not sure about that. I prefer the pure sci-fi book."

Lynn launched into a lecture. "*Romance* is a word used for entertainment—fantasy, adventure, medieval legends in verse involving chivalrous heroes on strange quests—"

"I know." He grinned. "I taught writing."

"You taught writing?" She gave him an intense look.

"Yes, I taught for two years so I could take this one off. I'm working on my Ph.D. and...uh...living at home, above the family drugstore in Anderson."

"Oh." That ended her lecture. Her writing "degree" was based on ten thousand books read and evaluated. Roughly ten thousand. Well, it had to have been a couple of thousand, anyway.

She asked it: "How old are you?"

"I'll be thirty in July."

"I have a younger brother about your age." He

was twenty-five, but by putting Kevin in the same league as her baby brother she hoped to kill off the beginnings of anything. What did she mean "beginnings"? She hurried on and pronounced, "I'm the eldest."

"How many kids are there?" He didn't look as if he'd received any message; he simply looked interested.

"Five."

'That must have made it tough," he speculated.

"Not especially. My dad took the night shift and my mom worked afternoons. One of them was home all the time."

"'Night shift'?" he asked.

"Dad made trucks. That was when International Harvester was still here in Fort Wayne. He didn't go to college. He and mom fell in love in high school, married when they graduated and started having babies."

"That's young to settle down."

"It wasn't bad. We had a good family life. They saw to it that all of us went to college. They're only in their early fifties now. They travel. They've been to Europe and South America, and they're going to China. They've got it made."

He nodded once in agreement. "I didn't have any brothers or sisters, but I was raised with one hundred eighty-seven cousins. Some of them live here in Fort Wayne, as a matter of fact. With all those cousins around, I never realized I had the potential to be a spoiled only child until I graduated from college. By then it was too late."

"'One hundred eighty-seven cousins'?"

He shrugged. "Give or take a couple of dozen."

"How many...actually?"

"I'll count them and tell you next time," he promised. "How long have you had a word processor?"

"About a year. Ed told me I should get one." She paused and enunciated clearly, "I work alone."

"I understand." He studied her for a moment. "Read my book at least? See how you like it?"

"Well...." She was reluctant.

"I know. We won't collaborate. But there's nothing to stop us from getting to know each other, is there?" He stood up. "I'll come back in a couple of days and we'll talk."

"No strings?"

"Of course not."

He left, and she resisted walking with him down to the street door. That would seem too friendly. But she peeked from her window and saw him get into his car and drive away. He had a very sassy little red car.

After he'd driven off, she turned away from the window and slowly went over to pick up the package that held his manuscript. She hefted it in her hands. It had to be most of the five hundred pages of a ream of paper. That was a long book. How would she ever get it read? Good Lord, what had Ed got her into? She did not have time to read some guy's book.

2

It was two o'clock in the morning when Lynn finished reading Kevin's book. Bleary-eyed, she stared at the clock and felt grumpy. It was an extremely good book, well plotted, well written, and the tension was so darn well-done that here it was, after two in the morning!

In a stupor, she went into the bathroom, refilled her hot-water bottle, got a drink and crawled back into bed, to go out like a light.

After that she pretended not to think about the book, but when her doorbell rang two days later she knew it was Kevin. She glanced out her window and wasn't at all surprised to see his red car parked at the curb.

She raced down the stairs, past the climbing people, and opened the door, congratulating herself for resisting the impulse to put on some makeup. That proved she was in control. She ignored reasoning why she felt she needed to be in control, or in control of what?

She said hello and attributed her surprising breathlessness to the stairs. He met her with the same startled look he'd given her the first time, and his lips parted as though he might speak. She figured he was shocked because she looked ghastly. Maybe so as not to offend aesthetic sensibilities she ought to comb her hair and put on a little makeup.

Of course, her hair was so short it didn't matter if she combed it or not. Self-consciously she ran her hand over her head, deliberately messing it up. Then she shook it as he grinned at her.

Since Lynn just stood there, Kevin put out a hand and pushed the door farther open, hesitated, then stepped toward her so that she had to move aside to avoid being crowded by him. He was bigger than she and loomed over her in the tiny entranceway. She was surprised when a squiggle of desire danced around in the pit of her stomach, and she thought how badly off she was if a total stranger could set off such a reaction.

She blurted out, "You can't kill off Tod." She hadn't meant to say that.

He didn't reply, but he was amused.

"In your book." She flung out a hand to help explain. "He can't die."

To guide her, Kevin took her arm which instantly tingled excitedly. Turning her to walk up the two flights, he said just a bit patronizingly, "A ray like that is excessively final."

"Couldn't it just wound him?" The tingle from his hand on her elbow had spread up her arm and was vibrating in her breast.

"That ray?" It was such an astonishing idea that he dropped his hand from her arm and paused to look at her.

Free of his touch, her arm began to calm down and

she spoke in the patient voice one used with a dense child who chooses not to understand. "Couldn't it just miss him?" And she even managed to gesture with the recovering arm.

In his own classroom voice, using his hands to illustrate, he explained, "You have to remember where they are. That bulkhead is wooden. If the ray hits it, it'll bring down the beams and that, of course, will change the whole situation. It would create a domino effect on events, and I'd have to rewrite the rest of the book." His look invited her to share in acknowledging the idiocy of that idea.

Having dismissed her suggestion, he reached past her to open the door, and they walked into her apartment. "Cleaning lady quit?" he asked sympathetically as he hung his coat on the hall tree.

With great patience, poorly projected, she persisted. "Tod doesn't have to die. He just disintegrated. There was no body to dispose of. He could still materialize later, alive." She sat down on the rocking chair.

He sat on the couch. "Why? What difference would that make? He's not important to the plot."

"But he'd be perfect for Claire," she declared.

"Tod?"

"Yes." She could barely control her impatience.

He shook his head dismissively. "He's bald."

"What's that got to do with anything?"

"Women like men with hair." His statement left no room for argument.

Undeterred, she challenged, "Who says? Men think they know all about women, but all they have are preconceived ideas about women. And they're generally wrong! Men think women envy them their—" She stopped as she realized she was over-reacting and getting herself into trouble. She gave him a quick glance, hoping he'd missed her dangling sentence.

In the silence that followed his eyes sparkled with amusement. "Their...." he encouraged her. She wasn't encouraged, so he prompted, "Their what?" He wasn't going to quit.

"You know."

"No." He pretended ignorance a bit too elaborately. "What? What do men think women envy?"

"Well, their... accoutrements?"

The laughter burst from him and continued immoderately. She waited with great endurance. When he'd quelled the sound of his hilarity and was only brimming with it, she stated, "Women also like bald men."

"I guess I'll have to take your word for it."

"So save Tod."

"Okay," he said in grudging capitulation. "I'll change the ray and just singe him."

"Don't hit anything vital," she cautioned.

He was still chuckling as he went to the door of her bedroom to examine his thick hair in her full-length mirror. Then he reached out and wiped a circle on the glass and raised censorious eyebrows toward her over the discernible circle left by his hand.

So naturally she snapped, "Worried about losing your hair?"

"Beside being a lousy housekeeper," he chided, "you have a definite mean streak."

"The apartment is only a little dusty," she defended herself. "I've been up to my ears in deadlines, correspondence, telephone calls and having to read some weirdo's sci-fi book."

"Great, isn't it?" He looked very sure of himself.

And grudgingly she admitted, "It's fantastic."

He accepted this with good grace and asked in turn, "Aren't you curious about how I liked yours?"

She gave him a cautious look.

Deliberately delaying a reply, he clasped his hands behind his back and looked at the ceiling. He pushed out that sensuous lower lip of his, then stepped over to the windows and stooped to look down at the street, giving the impression he sought kind words.

"Well?" she prodded.

He turned back to her and grinned. "Frankly, I was surprised. It's an excellent book. You write very well."

"Why, thank you."

"I have to admit I was just a tad disappointed. I thought romances were sexier." He shrugged. "This had an intricate story."

"To call a romance a sex book is like calling a body 'arms.' Arms are a part of the body. Sex is a part of romance."

"Was it autobiographical?"

She gave him a tight look. "Have you ever been in a spaceship or shot a ray gun?"

"No, not really."

"So? You do write about it."

"You've never made love?" He watched her closely.

"I was married for two years when I was nine-
teen."

"And divorced?" He had become very serious.

"Almost the minute Steve had his degree."

He nodded slowly in understanding. "So you
worked his way through college."

"And paid off his debts for 'our' future."

"There were a few of those guys at I.U. The di-
vorces came right after graduation. When did he
break it to you?"

Her reply was short. "The spring before he graduated."

"That's generally the time." He nodded with his
words.

"He told me I was a 'good kid' a lot and that I'd been
terrific, quitting school to support us. He said I was a
great typist—I did his papers, naturally—and he said
I'd always be able to support myself because I'd
learned so much and secretaries were always in demand and . . . oh, it's over. That was ten years ago."

"What happened to him?"

"He was debt free, and wife free, so he immediately married the girl back home. Her family was
better off than his." She didn't look at Kevin.

"It must have been hard on you. It's always a
shock to know there are people who deliberately set
out to use other people." His voice was low and
kind.

She lifted her chin. She would not have him feeling sorry for her; she only wanted him to know she

was immune now—manproof. "It's over," she said. "Save Tod for Claire."

"How'll that work?" He helped her to change the subject.

"They could become aware of each other during the stop at...how do you pronounce the asteroid supply depot?"

"'Aware'? They already know each other."

"Yes, but there isn't any awareness between them. The special looks, the accidental touching of hands or brushing against each other in the narrow corridors...."

"In space suits?" He was incredulous.

"On board."

"Yeah," he said thoughtfully as he considered that possibility. "I suppose so."

"When the alarm rings, because the switch malfunctions? They could both reach for it at once, and he could take her hand and hold it tightly. Then, after he's found the problem, he could realize that she'd been in danger. He could turn and look at her and they could both feel the chemistry."

"And he could drag her off to his sack in the sleeping closet."

She was doubtful about that but moved on to another subject.

"What about Brick? Captain Brick. Why 'Brick'? Why not Tom or Dick or Harry? 'Brick.'" She said the name with something of a snort.

"He's hard and tough and goes through things nicely. And he's good-hearted and in command. A brick of a man." He passed her a droll look.

So is Kevin. That vagrant thought flashed clearly
in Lynn's mind, and she studied him. Even having
met him only twice, she somehow knew it was true.
The realization was no more than a blink through
her mind when she became aware that Kevin was
still speaking.

"I was going to name him 'Force.' Guys can relate
to a name like Force. It sounds like a leader who can
get things done."

Lynn had to laugh and he shared it. She felt that
odd sensual wave rush through her body. It alarmed
her. Abruptly she picked up his manuscript. It was
neatly stacked with cardboard on both sides to protect the pages from the rubber bands. She stood and
handed it to him saying, "If you write all that in, it'll
be just fine."

"You have to help." He rose and accepted the
package.

"Just develop their awareness the way I suggested.
Take my book with you and use it as a guide. Tell it
in your own words." Her sentences were back to being short and jerky.

Straight-faced, he quoted in robot-spaced words:
"'He hit the panic button. As the alarms whooped
throughout the ship, he barked, "Ensign," and her
insides quivered.'"

"Maybe . . . not right then."

"When do her insides quiver?" he asked with ex-
aggerated interest.

"Afterward." She gave him a solemn look.

"After they make love? I'd think they'd get excited
beforehand," he commented guilelessly.

She assumed an extremely patient expression and enunciated, "After the emergency."

"He's been in space for three years! What could be more of an emergency than making love?"

"You are deliberately being obtuse. And I am not going to collaborate with you on this book." She walked over and pointedly opened the door to the stairs.

"You leaving?" He was amused again.

"You are," she replied flatly.

"I suppose I'll just have to try to write it all by myself." He sighed. "Would you read it and check it out?"

"If you want...." Now why had she said that? "Send it to Ed."

"That reminds me, he and Ann are quarreling again," he offered, as if to reopen the conversation.

"It isn't serious. They just like meeting someplace and making up. They're game players."

"Are you?" he asked quietly.

"A game player? Of course not. I'm out of that entirely," she stated emphatically.

He looked at her with a slight smile, then glanced down at his watch and back up at her. "I'll treat you to lunch," he offered generously. But then he slapped his pockets. "I'll be darned! I forgot my wallet. Uh...could you maybe spare a piece of bread and some peanut butter? It's such a long way back to Anderson." They eyed each other. He was relaxed; she was wary.

Knowing how he affected her senses, she was reluctant to have him around. She vacillated, then

gestured unwelcomingly and said, "It's in the kitch-
en."

"How innovative," he murmured as he took off
his sport jacket and hung it back on the hall tree by
the door. Then he unbuttoned his shirt cuffs to roll
up his sleeves. "Shall I make you one?"

Lynn had already escaped to her table where the
word processor sat, looking efficiently at the ready.
She was busy shuffling pages and so replied distractedly, "One what?"

"One peanut-butter sandwich," he spelled out.

"I'll eat the ham."

'You have ham?"

"You only asked if I had peanut butter. You didn't
ask if there was anything else," she replied defen-
sively.

"True," he agreed amicably as he went into the
kitchen.

Lynn began reading the last few pages she had
written, getting back into the mood of the story.
Coming from a family of seven, she had long ago
learned to block out any and all distractions as she
concentrated on what she was studying or reading.
The racket Kevin was making in the kitchen as he
concocted his peanut-butter sandwich faded away.

In her book the quarrel was over, her protagonists
were estranged and the woman was suffering from
their parting. Lynn knew about partings and suffering and she began to describe to the processor what
it was like and to remind herself about it as well.
Men could devastate lives. Men had wrecked her

twice now, and another male was there in her apartment. Kevin Walker.

He, too, was attractive and charming. He could be ruinous for her. Why had he been sent to disturb her life? She became so involved with her troubling thoughts that when Kevin came and stood by her she was startled—as if he'd just appeared out of a bottle.

"Lunch?" he inquired. "Or shall I wrap yours for later?"

"'Lunch'?" She was a little boggled by his nearness, and sharp twinges of excitement went skittering though her. The twinges had her attention, so she appeared vague.

"Yes, lunch. You know—the noon meal."

As if programmed, she pushed back her chair, got up and walked to the kitchen door, but she stopped there to exclaim, "You cleaned it!"

"Doesn't it look better?" He smiled, obviously pleased with himself, as he looked around the gleaming room.

"How dared you!" She turned to him angrily.

"Wha...?"

"I did not invite you to do this! I cannot have you coming in here and getting domestic—"

"I'm not getting domestic!" he objected. "I was trying to prevent ptomaine poisoning!"

"It wasn't that dirty!" She was indignant.

'I suppose those molds in the refrigerator were scientific experiments?" He raised his brows.

"You cleaned the refrigerator?" She went over

and yanked it open. It was almost empty. There was one egg in the egg basket, a bottle of lemon juice, five bottles of salad dressing, two of catsup, some dill pickles and a gallon of milk.

Conversationally he said, "One lump I figured had to have been a tomato at one time—because of the seeds," he elaborated. "I can only assume the rest was also of the vegetable category."

"The dishes are all washed, too," she exclaimed. "Where did you put them all?"

"I threw away half," he replied matter-of-factly.

"You wouldn't have."

"No, of course not." He opened the cupboard. "Since you don't collect canned goods, there was plenty of room."

"There's always milk and flour. I make my own bread." She was back on the defensive.

"You make it? I saw it was homemade and it's delicious, but I assumed someone gave it to you."

"Food isn't important to me," she informed him stubbornly as she involuntarily obeyed his motion for her to go over to the neatly set table. He held one of the two chairs for her and she sat down.

There were sandwiches, pickles, potato chips, and by each plate was a glass of milk. He sat down next to her, and in spite of her indignation, all on its own, her body reacted to being so close to his.

"Where'd all this food come from?"

"I went out for most of it—including the milk, which you claimed you always had but didn't. And there was no coffee at all!"

"I don't drink coffee," she informed him.

"Figures. No coffee drinker is ever out of coffee. How in the world do you survive?"

"Without coffee?" she asked. "Easy. I don't like it."

"That's un-American. But there wasn't any food."

"There's tea...."

"Not very nourishing. I'm surprised you're so nicely shaped. I found your jogging outfit hanging next to the broom. It's a wonder you're not shaped like one."

"Don't try to mother me," she warned.

"Mothering is a long way from—" He stopped and then said sternly, "You have to eat better."

"Who decides what's 'better'? There are those who live to eat and those who eat to live. I eat to live. Food bores me."

He leaned his head back to look at her dispassionately through those thick eyelashes as he concluded, "You probably don't have any taste buds."

"Of course I have taste buds. I eat pizza and chili and other things."

"That's a terrible diet!" he pronounced. "You need fish and vegetables and fresh fruit."

"I do not! Just because you're a live-to-eater, don't try to change my life."

"Not your life," he corrected. "Just your diet. Since you have no taste buds, you'll have to be trained to appreciate good food. That's something sensitive people come by naturally. They're born with refined tastes."

"You're accusing me of being insensitive?" She was chewing furiously.

"Oh, no," he soothed. "Just more . . . basic."

They sat crammed together, chewing. Her breathing had quickened with her temper. He had arranged his mouth to avoid laughing, and she had the strong impression he was enjoying himself. She swallowed and blotted her lips, then told him authoritatively, "When you mature, you won't be so argumentative."

He stopped chewing, swallowed and replied, "You make a statement, I respond, and you call it arguing?"

"See?" she said in a superior way. "I rest my case."

"You're autocratic," he stated, lifting his eyebrows so that she again caught a glimpse through his lashes of very amused gray eyes.

"You are attacking my character." She waved her arms and he protected her glass of milk. "And my housekeeping . . ." she sputtered.

"I was merely pointing out areas for improvement," he replied judiciously.

"There is no way I could ever collaborate with you." She spaced the words carefully, but Kevin was already off and running.

"Why don't you provide the place for us to work," he proposed. "And I'll keep it clean and do the cooking—if you'll continue to bake the bread. It's the best I've ever had."

"Don't try to weasel around and make things right."

"What's wrong?" He appeared mildly surprised.

Suddenly she asked, "Where did you get the money for the groceries?"

"I uh...."

"You said you didn't have any money," she accused. "And you couldn't survive until you got back home, and did I have some peanut butter? Okay. Where did you get the money?"

"I'm thinking!" he replied crossly. "Imaginative space writing doesn't lend itself to ordinary, everyday situations. I have to have time to figure something out."

"You had your wallet all along!" she exclaimed.

"Very good." He praised. "You're quick!"

"Why didn't you just go out and eat?" she demanded stridently. "Why try to trick me?"

He smiled at her but did not reply. She felt that delightful, scary rippling sensation again and she hitched her chair minutely away from his.

He was still very close because there wasn't really enough room for two chairs. And her breasts decided to push against her sweater. She lifted her chin, protectively defiant, and tried to exhale enough to make them less obvious. She put the arm closest to him up on the table to partially conceal her body, but then he turned away, back toward the window, and put his arm along the table in front of him so his shoulder was pressing against hers.

Lynn jerked backward in her chair to break the electric contact, and Kevin looked around his shoulder at her. She was sure he knew exactly what sweet turmoil he had stirred up in her silly body.

3

IT WAS ALMOST A WEEK before he came by again. Although Lynn had had no intention of going down and opening the door she found herself doing just that. But she didn't smile and she was proud of her composure. "Yes?" she said, pretending he was a salesman whose product could not possibly interest her.

"Hi," he greeted her cheerfully, as if welcome. "Miss me?" Handing her a manilla envelope, he turned away, still chatting. "Mind the door. I'll bring in the wood."

"'The wood'?" She couldn't slam the door; she had his manuscript. She couldn't pitch it outside. No author could ever do anything destructive to someone else's work. He had very neatly trapped her.

Kevin went to his car and opened the trunk, which was filled with neatly split wood. She watched him as he stacked one arm too full. Then he slammed the trunk closed, adjusted the load into both arms and walked rapidly to her. She had no choice but to hold the door wide open and get out of his way.

The next thing she knew they were in her apartment. He had a fire going in the fireplace and she was sitting on the sofa, his manuscript on her lap, feeling very cozy. She was again in a loose nondescript sweat shirt and jeans, while he had selfishly covered his body with a navy sweater and cream cords.

He straightened, admired his fire, then peered around critically. "Well, you haven't wrecked complete havoc in the week I've left you alone."

She gave him a baleful glare.

"But how are you eating? What do you have in your refrigerator?" Even as he spoke he strode across the room into the kitchen and opened the refrigerator door. There was silence. He closed the door and returned to stand over her. "You've made fresh bread," he said accusingly.

Deliberately misinterpreting his words, she replied, "I ran out."

"You know, that's the only change," he scolded.

"You're not my keeper," she snapped back.

"I believe temper is the only thing that puts roses in your cheeks. If you ate properly, your disposition would improve."

"It would not!" She struggled to extricate herself from the depths of the couch.

"It wouldn't? You mean you're locked into this one?" He appeared amazed.

"Listen. I want you to take your book and leave!"

He looked at his watch and the phone rang. "Ah," and he sighed in relief. "Saved by the bell." He picked up her phone and simply handed it to her.

"Hello, love." It was Ed. "How're things going? How's the book?"

"Mine is going well," she replied in a stilted tone. "I'm almost finished."

"That's great. They like it as usual and they're buying. But I'm really interested in Kevin's. Have you started work on that?"

"No." Then she enunciated, "I work alone."

There was a pithy silence before Ed grated, "Why are you making this so hard for me?"

"Why are you making this so impossible for me?" she countered.

"You can ask that when you're spending the money and signing autographs at a world premier of the film. Let me talk to Kevin."

Silently she handed the phone to Kevin, who thanked her cheerfully. She pretended not to listen, but she might just as well have left the room, because Kevin made only monosyllabic sounds and chortled a lot.

Then it occurred to her. How had Ed known Kevin was going to be there? He hadn't asked if Kevin was there. He'd said, "Let me speak to Kevin." She narrowed her eyes and studied the man.

And what a man he was. His body was hard and athletic. He wore his clothes well. They fitted him nicely and he looked comfortable in them. He had a casual, masculine grace.

She looked at his big, capable, square hands with their long fingers. His hands were rough. He'd split that wood. He was really marvelous.

His voice rumbled in his chest as he talked to Ed, and his laugh was throaty and very attractive. Just then he glanced up and caught her watching him. His smile was sexy as sin.

Finally he handed the phone back to her with a wicked grin. "Ed wants to talk to you."

She put the phone to her ear and with grim resolve began, "Ed—"

"Lend your brilliance to this book. There's no one else we can turn to. You are the best. Be kind. You'll be the making of the boy. He's a quick learner. All you have to do is uncork his genius. He's so talented—he'll be fine once you've given him some direction. You'll never regret it. It'll bring your books a whole new audience. My other lines are blinking. I'll be in touch. Bye," and he hung up.

Lynn raised her eyes to the thickly lashed horizontals of Kevin's and said, "I think he was reading everything he said."

"He probably had someone else write it. Did he leave you a way out?"

She shook her head as she hung up the phone.

"Me, neither." He sounded satisfied as he lowered himself onto the sofa cushions next to her with a plop. "You'll get a curvature from this thing. It doesn't support your back properly."

"Good Lord!" she exclaimed in exasperation. "Okay, okay, let's get this over with."

He took the envelope, opened it and eagerly pulled out a sheaf of papers. "I put in a scene at the supply depot the way you said. The idea is that Tod wanted to be sure they had the ice guns and Claire goes with him. So there they are alone, she stumbles and he grabs her to keep her from falling. How's that?" Kevin looked expectantly at Lynn.

"How did she stumble?" Lynn frowned, trying to visualize it.

"Deliberately?" His smile came back.

"Are the space suits bulky?"

"Not especially." He was watching her mouth and her body noticed.

"Then when he catches her he could slide his hand up her side?" She swallowed rather noisily.

His voice went deep and he licked his lower lip. "You mean he gets to grope her right away?"

"How ... how long have they known each other?" She tried for a clinical approach. "You said something about three years?"

"He's been traveling three years in that ship. She's new crew. An engineer."

"An ensign."

"Young." He nodded. "Now I prefer older women." He lifted his chin knowingly as his glance slid over to her. He wasn't talking about his book anymore.

Lynn understood his meaning and said firmly, "No." She'd better make that clear.

"Collaborators always have affairs." He turned one hand palm up, as if offering a glimpse of their unavoidable fate.

Her body quivered for agreement but reason asserted itself and she said in a relatively steady voice, "We aren't collaborators. You keep your distance."

"All truly great authors have open minds," he offered.

"My mind is open." The words were right, but her mind was so open it was entertaining a vivid picture of Kevin and her. She struggled to rise from the sofa. With a hand to her bottom he gave her a boost, and she turned on him again, warning, "Keep your distance."

Nodding solemnly, he replied, "I'll watch for a stumble."

She flung up her arms in exasperation as she walked around the cozy living room with its warm colors, crackling fire and dangerous man. "This isn't going to work!"

"We could have him accidentally get into her cocoon in the sleeping capsule." He pretended to believe she meant the book was being difficult.

She pivoted, her imagination captured by the problem. "I thought the sleeping envelopes fitted only one person."

"She's small," he ventured.

"I don't see how you're going to work this out. The gravity and pressure and the crowding are maddening." She clutched her hair. So was he maddening.

"Yeah," Kevin agreed. "Poor guys. It's really tough. That's why sci-fi writers always find them an earthlike planet."

She halted in midpace and perked up. "Could we find one?" She'd said "we," and he smiled on hearing it.

"Well...." He sounded very doubtful. "I suppose we could stumble across a small one."

"That would help enormously."

"There'd be humanlike inhabitants so old Brick could do a little dallying with the princess. Captains always have relationships—which are thwarted after a time—with the female ruler or the ruler's daughter. Captains never fall in love, however briefly, with ordinary women."

"You sound derisive," Lynn accused.

"Oh, no!" He was emphatic. "I love sci-fi. And I believe, given the chance, I could learn to love romance, as well. Try me."

Try him which way, she wondered in a rush of electric sensation. It would be fantastic to dally with Kevin. But she suggested, "Let's find the small, earthlike planet."

"With a blue sun."

"Good heavens, no! Blue light isn't at all flattering to a woman. Tod would be revolted by Claire under a blue light."

"Not right away. After all, it's been three years."

"And never in all that time...?" She couldn't manage to complete the question.

"It's a little like the first explorers who set out from Europe. Except that after you leave this planet the seas of space are very, very wide and empty and the ports are few and far between."

"Why go?" she asked softly, feeling as if she were standing on shore watching a ship vanish over a lonely horizon into the unknown. A ship with Kevin Walker on board.

"Why go? Curiosity."

She realized Kevin was an adventurer. "Would you go into space?" She really wanted to know.

His reply was quick. "Next year."

"Why next year?" she asked. "Why not now?"

"I have a few things to do before then." He stood up without the struggle she'd had fighting free of the sofa cushions.

"The book?" she whispered, watching him move toward her.

"Along with the book." His voice was husky as he came to her and stood there looking down at her. He was so intent she could see the gray pools of his eyes, and her breathing was affected. Her lips parted as he took her into his arms and brought her body close to his. And then he kissed her.

She'd written about drowning in kisses, but she'd never before experienced it. A tide of feeling flooded through her, touching secret places and setting off such a sensual deluge that she was conscious of nothing but her need for him.

So she clung to him, his mouth her lifeline. Grabbing handfuls of his sweater, pressing against him, she was grateful for the bands of his arms that helped mold her body very close to his hard masculine strength.

Kevin raised his mouth minutely, then deliberately brushed her lips with his. His voice was husky. "We have to find that small, earthlike planet."

She looked up at him unsteadily, her body still reacting to him outrageously. When he spoke again she felt his deep voice rumble in her own chest.

"Your eyes are the color of sherry, and they make me a little drunk."

Since his eyelashes had a similar effect on her, she could understand the feeling, so she nodded sympathetically before jerking herself back to reality. She gasped and pushed against him. Reluctantly he released her, then immediately became very brisk and businesslike—as if he hadn't just participated in an utterly devastating, mind-bending kiss.

"May I?" he said, indicating her typewriter.

Her head moved a little loosely, for she was still somewhat mesmerized. He took the movement for agreement, found paper, sat down and began to type. He typed very well.

Lynn stood there, abandoned in the middle of the floor, wanting more than kisses. She cast around the room for help, for something to save her from this madness. She needed to get away from him and clear her head.

She stumbled into the kitchen, took her jogging suit from behind the back door, drifted into the bedroom and put it on. As she left the apartment, he briefly lifted a hand, not speaking.

Her mind far outdistanced her legs as she jogged the course. It was bitterly cold, and she had to stop and do jumping jacks to keep her blood warm as she went over her problem. Her problem was Kevin. If she wasn't careful, she could be smitten. What she needed was a defense plan.

The trouble was that while she thought of how to keep him at arm's length, what she really wanted was more. More kisses. More of Kevin. And as she jogged through the park and stopped to do the various exercises, her mind took her with him to the planet with the blue sun.

At her regular spot she automatically slowed

down to begin cooling off. With continuing automation, she whistled under Mrs. Hobbs's window and watched until the drape waggled, before she allowed herself to return to her own apartment.

She wasn't much better off for the jogging workout because she knew Kevin would be there in her apartment when she got back. She was torn between reluctance to arrive and the desire to hurry home to him. To *him*. A small inner voice warned; *pay attention, Lynn.*

When she walked into the living room, he was riffling through some pages, but he looked up and grinned at her. "Need some help with your shower?" he asked as if offering to open a stubborn jar.

She didn't bother to reply. But as she showered she was very conscious of being naked and that he was only two thin doors away. She sighed, exasperated by her own thoughts. She really had to stop this ridiculous fantasizing about a man she had no intention of getting involved with. No one was going to mess up her life again. She was her own person now.

But she put on her best purple sweater and white slacks and ran a sensuous pinky-purple lipstick over her mouth.

As she returned her jogging suit to its peg, Kevin glanced up at her and gave a soft whistle of appreciation. She lifted her nose and walked on by without saying anything. What could she say that would sound sensible? "You look pretty good to me, too, so get out"?

When she returned to the living room, there was determination in her step. "I believe it would be best if we each wrote separately. We could—"

"With a blue sun," he mused, "the plants would be orange. Is that too jarring?"

"No." She stopped to consider. "It wouldn't all be orangy orange. There would be as much variation in the oranges as there are in the greens here on earth."

"Excellent!" He grinned in approval.

"Just brilliant."

"'Brilliant.'" He watched her with an amused look and added softly, "And beautiful."

"As I was saying, I believe it would be better if we worked separately—" She spoiled the statement by swallowing in the middle of it.

Agreeably he replied, "Okay. I'll use the typewriter and you use the processor."

"And just phone the situation or questions," she completed her thought.

"I like it here." He was definite. "This is a lot more inspiring than the apartment, uh, the place over the drugstore." His eyes shifted around the room for a moment but finally settled on her and rested there. "I find you're very...."

His voice was a soft growl. "I'm very what?"

"Distracting." The word was muffled.

Positively beaming, he got eagerly to his feet. "I drive you to distraction?"

"That's not what I meant." She warded him off with a hand and blushed because her words were a lie. "I mean, I find it distracting to have another person here. I'm used to working alone."

"Don't worry," he soothed. "You'll get used to me."

"No. I really—"

"What's for lunch?" Briskly he covered the typewriter, crossed the living room, walked into the kitchen and opened the refrigerator door.

"Eggs!" he called. "How about an omelet? We should use up the tomatoes, anyway."

He'd said "we" as if they were a pair. She felt a little desperate. From the kitchen door she tried one more time. "I...."

"Here, mate, into the galley and slice the bread."

"Mate"? What sort of "mate"? In a near swoon she took up the knife to slice a loaf of her bread, as he began chopping up the vegetables, and then she set the table. She was excessively aware of him, of sharing that small space. It was as if his body emitted a stimulating charge that had a potent affect on her nerve endings.

The butter melted in the omelet pan and Kevin poured in the beaten eggs. He concentrated on the skillet then, but when he slid the omelets onto their plates he smiled at her companionably, in a cozy sort of way.

At that moment she wished he'd pitch the omelet pan over into the sink, take her into his arms and make love to her. That unbidden thought forced her to clench her fists and grit her teeth to keep herself from assaulting him. What in the world was happening to her?

Woodenly she sat down at the table and again the shoulder to shoulder closeness sent a wild sensual current coursing through her. It played havoc with her senses, and she realized that Kevin was indeed desirable, delectable—potentially devastating.

That night, lying alone in her bed, Lynn decided that the only smart thing to do was to have one of her nieces or a nephew with her each day as a chaperon. That was the thing to do. And some time toward morning, she finally fell asleep.

She dreamed of a small planet with a blue sun and of Mark. He was making love to a blonde whose long hair turned orange and whose lips turned a gawdy purple. But then the two became Kevin and Lynn and they writhed together in passionate embraces and it was lovely.

IN THE DAYS that followed, Lynn found she could hardly wait for Kevin's next visit. *Fool*, she scolded herself. But she anticipated seeing him with an almost brainless excitement.

It wouldn't hurt for her to be with him, she rationalized, to look at him and listen to him. All she had to do was to contain herself so he wouldn't suspect how much she was attracted to him.

She was in control and she could do that. She just wanted to look at him. Only to look. Not to touch.

LYNN FOUND IT WAS EASY to write Tod and Claire's love story. It was easy to describe the need and hunger, the agony of unfulfilled love they endured before finding that little earthlike planet. There they were finally able to shed their protective suits and everything else. It was Tod and Claire who made wild, exquisite love for enchanted pages, but to Lynn it was Kevin and she who inhabited their bodies. How shocking... and she smiled.

Brick's encounter with the ship's psychiatrist was flaming and erotic but not as much fun for Lynn to write. She was stuck on how to make the analytical psychiatrist blossom enough to attract and accept the advances of the macho Brick. Brick didn't really appeal to Lynn and she complained to Kevin, "He's impossible!"

"He's in charge. He can't be frivolous." Kevin dismissed any changes in his hero.

"I think the psychiatrist beds him only to see if it might relax his iron spine. Or to see if he's capable of doing something so human." She thought for a minute, frowning at an innocent plant. Then she exploded with inspiration. "Can she get pregnant?"

"They're all sterilized for the duration of the voyage because pregnant women and babies would only complicate everything. Think of diapers and burping a kid and space suits for them and...it's out of the question." He frowned at the tiny, one-and-a-half-year-old niece who was stacking blocks in front of the screened fireplace. "I didn't know you babysat so much."

"If you think babies on a spaceship are a problem, you should try them in a small house during winter here on earth."

He observed the engrossed niece. "She gets along all right. What's the fuss?"

"Her older brother is at my mother's today, and another sister has the baby. That way each kid gets some individual attention and gets used to being away from home before they go to school. And my sister gets some relief."

"'Relief'? That doesn't sound as if she's very maternal."

"There you go again! Why do men consider themselves authorities on things they know absolutely nothing about? Things they've researched in clinics—observation instead of involvement. They say, 'What have *we* here?' Then they say, 'That doesn't hurt,' and, 'It's nerves.' They tell a mother of five children she needs some bedrest without telling her how to accomplish it."

"You're anti-MD," he hypothesized.

She shrugged dismissively. "They come in handy now and then."

"I dropped out of medical school." Kevin had

made a mature choice and redirected his life with only brief regret.

"Why?" she asked cautiously.

"I took on the symptoms of my patients. I was sick all the time and it was just empathy."

"You'll make a dreadful husband."

"I'll be fantastic!" he argued.

"No." She shook her head. "When your wife gets sick, you will, too. She'll have to drag herself out of bed and tend to you, and you won't even really be sick. You'll probably go into labor with her, as well."

"That is true," he admitted. "When I was in med school, there was a bad fog and more than fifty cars were in a terrible pileup on the highway. Even the medical students were pressed into service. I rode a police car out, and I barely knew more than the cops.

"One woman went into early labor." He shook his head once slowly, remembering. "And I shared it with her, every contraction, every gasping breath, and we gave birth to a darling little girl." His smile was broad and his pleasure genuine. "They named her 'Charlene.' My middle name is 'Charles,'" he explained, trying to sound offhand.

She knew her expression was very tender. Too tender. So to counteract it she reached out and ruffled his thick brown hair. But he caught her arm, fell back to the sofa and tumbled her onto his lap. She gasped as much from surprise as from the sensation that shook her when she felt his hard body beneath hers.

It felt as if liquid honey were flowing through her body—very warm, very sweet. And she knew it would not do at all. She had to get away from him.

She struggled and he laughed. Effortlessly he controlled her, allowing her movement but confining her to his lap. "Let...me...go!" she grunted.

Her niece chortled and abandoned her blocks to join in the fun. Climbing the sofa wasn't easy for her and Kevin had to lend a hand, which he did while still controlling Lynn's movements. Then the tot confidently crawled over the cushions, plopped down on top of Lynn and made herself at home.

Her lap thus occupied, Lynn had to quit struggling, though she was still panting from the exertion. As Kevin made the two on his lap comfortable her niece jabbered with satisfaction and laughed, enjoying the frolic.

Kevin's attention was caught by the babbling and he exclaimed, "Listen! It's Martian!"

Lynn looked around. "What is?"

"She speaks Martian!" He was astounded.

Lynn said, "So that's it. We did wonder. Her brother understands her."

"It's not street Martian," he explained. "It's the formal diplomatic tongue, like Castilian Spanish with the lisp."

"She does lisp," Lynn admitted.

"The lisp will probably disappear when she switches to English. It's simply the demands of the form she speaks."

"Where'd she learn it?" Lynn challenged his imagination.

"She's probably part Martian." He looked thoughtful. "Has your sister ever mentioned having had any encounters in her sleep? It was probably the contact of a landing party. If your sister looks like you, their leader probably thought she was a princess—"

"And his name was the Martian version of Brick or Force and he dallied with my sister, but the relationship was thwarted...."

"Naturally!" Kevin made it appear as though she'd stated the obvious.

"And he flew off in his spaceship, leaving my sister forlorn and pregnant."

"She wouldn't actually remember," he reminded Lynn. "There's the kiss of forgetfulness."

"Oh, yes," she acknowledged. "But we have little Princess Brick here." Lynn lay against Kevin's chest, her head on his shoulder, his arms around her, her niece on her lap. She reached over and played with the downy wisps of curls over the baby's ears and was glad the child was there to receive the smiles and touches she wanted to give to Kevin.

The princess raised her tiny silken eyebrows and strung together a series of foreign-sounding words.

Kevin exclaimed, "I'll bring my tape recorder, and we'll decipher it. We'll break the code and know the secrets of Mars! She's the Rosetta Stone of the Martian civilization."

Lynn looked up at him and he brought his face down to within inches of hers. She was instantly paralyzed by an onslaught of thrills. She had to swallow before she could parrot, "'Secrets of Mars'?"

He agreed in a low voice that vibrated from his chest into her shoulder and breast and sent her whole nervous system into a sensual swoon.

It was fascinating to look at him at such close

range. She wished she'd put on some mascara. She did have eyelashes, but they were nothing compared to his.

The princess said, "Meow, bowwow, moo."

Kevin gasped, "See? We're contaminating her language already!"

Lynn wanted an excuse to look back up at him so she said placidly, "You're just a little strange."

That startled him, and he raised his eyebrows to exclaim, "I am? I always thought it was everyone else." Then he said positively, "I am normal. It's you."

"What's me?" Lynn was only minimally aware they spoke over and through priceless reams of Martian coming from the princess, wasting the opportunity to understand.

"Our agent is probably a Martian plant," Kevin postulated. "Ed's been instructed by his superiors to corrupt me because I'm too close to the truth. So he recruited you to sway my emotions and distract me from my cause, which is learning that the Martians have landed."

"'The Martians have landed'?" That did surprise her a bit.

"Now you'll scoff and tell me I'm crazy, and if I continue to spread the word you'll sign my commitment. I'll rot in a padded cell, driven raving mad by frustrated lust."

"'Lust'?" She was confused. "I thought your frustration would be from your thwarted attempt to spread the word of the landings."

"You're trying to make me believe you're un-knowing." He kissed her, making her toes curl and her breasts rise against him. Raising his head and looking down at her seriously for a minute, he commended, "You're doing a fabulous job of it—distracting me, seducing me. What sort of acknowledgement do Martians give? Do you have newspapers, TV? Will you be interviewed? Will you yawn and say, 'He was easy'?"

"I'll say—" she considered "—I'll say, 'Which one?'"

"You shameless Martian hussy!" He squeezed her and she gasped as her body reacted to him.

The princess rode the shift of their bodies, but both of them put out hands to be sure of her balance. Kevin demanded, "To how many men have you played the red herring when they've come close to the truth about saucer landings? Just how many men have you lured from their bounden duty?"

"This year?" she inquired politely.

He kissed her again, sending a stab of tormenting desire through her. His free hand slid up inside the back of her sweater on her bare skin, and her breathing shut down as he caressed her sweetly.

He lifted his mouth as they both gasped for air. Then he kissed her again, his tongue touching hers, the kiss fusing. His hand slid smoothly around under her arm and closed over her bare breast. Her mind tilted a bit and the prude in her pointed out that he had his hand on her bare breast and why hadn't she worn a bra?

The princess stood up on their laps and tried to join their kiss. She laughed the delicious laughter of a small child truly amused.

While Lynn kept a firm handful of the princess's corduroys to keep her from tumbling, she was actually hypnotized by Kevin's kisses, his nearness, the sound of his disturbed breathing, his intent eyes and his caressing hand. She looked down at her chest, then looked up at Kevin and raised her eyebrows inquiringly. Her conscience observed sarcastically that she wasn't doing anything about his wandering hand and why wasn't she?

"Your surface is very different from mine," he said huskily.

And she laughed. So did the princess. Then Kevin kissed Lynn again. Quick, hungry kisses. But her mood was broken, and the princess was complaining she wasn't getting her share. Kevin turned and kissed her tiny nose, but he didn't move his hand from Lynn's chest. And she didn't, either. She liked having his hand there, slowly savoring her with hot strong fingers.

The princess became bored with them and slid down from the sofa on her stomach. Lynn needlessly leaned to guide her, but Kevin's hand clung to her and his other hand, freed of the obligation of the baby's safety, came to her hip. He pulled her across him as he again sought her mouth to kiss her without the distraction of the child.

Lynn could not resist. Not right away. She wanted it as much as he, and she was briefly pliant in his arms, her mouth eagerly cooperative as his kiss searched and tormented. When she reluctantly began to resist, he coaxed, but she was insistent and he finally released her, though not giving up altogether. He tempted and cajoled with honeyed kisses and sweet touches and gentle hugging. But she managed to get away.

She stood up and felt giddy, as if the floor weren't quite steady. She put her hands to her head to be sure it wouldn't float away. Then she disguised the movement by finger-combing her short hair. She untwisted and pulled down her sweater and adjusted the waistband of her slacks as she walked several steps away from him. By then she could look at him, one quick peek, and after that she took several glances, but she couldn't handle a steady look.

He could. He sat there, his knees apart, his arms spread to his sides on the sofa cushions, his hands palms down but clenched and his face very serious. His breathing was quick and shallow, and his gaze was steady on her. He looked very dangerous. Deliciously dangerous—a desirable, aroused man. Not violently ravishing, or rapine, but one very capable of convincing an unwary woman she wanted his way.

She was surprised to find herself sidling cautiously away, being careful how she moved, holding her body formally straight and not daring to breathe. She leaned down and picked up the princess. Then she turned and looked at Kevin.

He rolled up from the sofa in a fluid uncurling motion, and it was awesome to see such muscle control. Her stomach quivered. It was very like being in a room with a pet tiger and suddenly realizing it might forget it was tamed.

He came over and took them both in his arms. "The princess is no protection, Lynn," he said, and kissed her in such a way Lynn was sure steam was rising from her body. The princess's comments and questions barely penetrated her passion-crazed mind, but the thought did occur to her that very small children were not much of a prophylactic.

When Kevin had completed his sensual work of art and lifted his head, she knew she'd fogged up the entire room, because his face wasn't clear. She blinked and reminded herself to breathe.

He released the princess from their arms and stood her on the floor while he steadied Lynn's balance. The room wasn't clouded after all, it was just that her eyes couldn't focus.

But when he straightened and would have taken Lynn back into his arms, her writer's mind rescued her. "Sir?" she asked. "Who are you?" And she dramatically put her hand to her forehead. "Who am I? What is this place? Who is that child?"

He put his hands on his hips and said, "The kiss of forgetfulness only makes you forget I've made love to you."

"Did you?" She did a very commendable job sounding confused.

"No...not yet."

Her knees almost buckled. "If you were an earthling, you wouldn't know about the kiss of forgetfulness! You're the Martian. That's why you recognized the princess's speech."

"Any really good sci-fi writer can recognize Martian speech," he scoffed. "You don't have to be Spanish to recognize that language."

"But you not only recognized the princess's speech," she reminded him, "you did give me the kiss of forgetfulness."

"How do you remember all that?" He smiled slightly.

"What?"

"Well, this." He took a quick step forward, bashed his head on the undertrough of the ceiling's dip.

As he hit his head, she exclaimed and lifted her hands in a protective gesture. He reached out and gathered her close, tightening his arms until their bodies were crushed together and his mouth closed over hers. Her hands fluttered helplessly, uselessly in the air, so she brought them to his poor head and held it gently.

When he breathed, she asked softly, "Are you okay?"

"Not yet," he said in a tight voice. His body was rigid and his hands trembled as he held her plastered against him.

"I think you may have a concussion. Can you see?" She was getting worried.

"Only you."

She moved her hands gently on his head. "Does it hurt?"

"Badly."

She nodded. "A concussion."

"Frustration," he corrected.

"You ran into the ceiling," she pointed out. "It's

the eyelashes. I'll bet it's like living in a thicket." Her fingers smoothed his eyebrows.

He widened his eyes, and Lynn looked into the gray depths. She smiled, then remembered herself and stiffened as she pried his hands from her and wriggled away.

"You're supposed to be teaching me romance," Kevin reminded her.

"To write romance."

"How can I write it without experiencing it?" He slowly, relentlessly followed her retreat.

Still backing, Lynn said, "If you go on like this, I won't open the door for you again."

"I could have the key copied," he offered. "It is a nuisance for you to run down two flights of stairs. With a key I could come and go—"

"I mean it." She was firm. "If you have any need—"

"I do. I do," he groaned.

"For me to help you with that book," she finished, then scolded, "You will have to behave yourself. No more fooling around."

"You didn't like it?"

Now what was she supposed to say? And be believed? "It's unprofessional."

"Well, I haven't ever actually been paid for my kisses so I probably can't be called a real pro, but I might be able to get a few references...."

"I mean it," she declared. "No more. I will not get involved."

"You drive me wild," he growled, and the timbre

of his voice sent tremors through her body. And they weren't even touching this time.

She braced herself against her reaction to him and commanded, "Control yourself!" as she struggled to control herself.

"But you do admit you drive me wild?"

"I believe you're undisciplined." She was extremely pleased with finding that word.

"'Undisciplined'? Me?" Kevin deliberately contemplated Lynn's entire body, making a shiver go up her back and down the undersides of her arms.

Just then the princess looked up and said urgently, "An' Lynn, pottie!"

As if triggered to fire, Lynn scooped her up and fled to the bathroom, thinking maybe it was a good thing she'd had the baby around, after all. She would have to be very careful—be sure one of the kids was always here and be professional and aloof with Kevin. The "looking but not touching" wasn't working.

When the two females emerged from the privacy of the bath, Kevin observed unkindly, "Isn't she a little old not to be housebroken?"

"At least she told me." Lynn dismissed his ignorance. "I suggest the next—" What should she call it? Encounter? Episode? "The next time Claire and Tod...." She paused again. How could she speak of making love?

"What." He grinned, enjoying her blush.

She looked at him coolly, pretending that her blush was a reflection of the firelight. "There should

be another love scene about a hundred pages later,"
she said.

He picked up his manuscript and flipped to the
designated spot. "The men and the two women are
in separate holding areas, in chains, held by the en-
emy in the bottom of a snake cave, and you say it's
time for another love scene? How are they going to
solve that?"

"I don't know and I have to work on my own
book. You go home and figure that out. Then mail it
to me, and I'll look it over."

"You're going to send me out in this storm?" He
was shocked.

She hurriedly glanced out the window and saw
the shimmer of tiny ice crystals floating in the air.
She looked at Kevin. "Just because the air is con-
densing into ice flakes doesn't mean it's cold."

"It doesn't? My God, woman, what does it mean,
then? If the very air is turning into ice? Just like
your heart?"

"Go home," she directed.

"Rejection. My psyche will never recover. My
character will be warped and people will say, 'Whatever happened to that pleasant young man? What
could have turned him into such a recluse?' And no
one will know it was because of a hard-hearted
woman who threw me out in the cold of winter
when the very air was turning into ice . . . rejected."

"That was lousy writing," she critiqued objec-
tively.

"I always rewrite. The second version will tear

your heart out. Not that you'd ever miss it." He gave her a hurt glance, his lower lip stubborn.

With an elaborate sigh she told him, "It will be a great help when you turn thirty."

"I'll lose my baby fat?" He tilted his head to study her.

On their own, her eyes went down his lean, hard body. He didn't have an ounce of fat. Her eyes went back to his face, and behind those eyelashes he might have been looking at her with some smugness. He had to know his body was fantastic.

He strolled over to the door and took his coat from the rack. Putting it on, he said, "Call me if you need me for anything. Groceries, sex, firewood, sex, a stuck window, sex...."

"That window!" She flung out an arm toward it. "Could you unstick it?"

His manner was cocky as he swaggered over, tested the window, banged the frame several times and opened it with little effort. "Anything else? A squeaky hinge, a kiss-starved mouth?" he asked as he lowered the window back into place.

She shook her head, her face a little flushed but serious. "Kevin, I mean it. I must not get involved with you."

"Don't worry, Lynn." He was very sincere and kind. "I won't quit trying, but I won't be unreasonable. We'll just take it easy." He started for the door, stopped, snapped his fingers and came back to her. He took firm hold of her shoulders, preventing her retreat, and gave her a hard, thorough kiss. He raised his head and said, "The kiss of forgetfulness, so you won't brag." Then he turned and left.

She stood there, leaning her bottom against the back of the sofa, trying to gather her wits as she listened to his steps rattle down the stairs. She heard the front door open and close. And he was gone.

5

HE DIDN'T COME BACK for five and a half days. She'd even dispensed with the child chaperon on the fourth day, thinking that would bring him, but it hadn't worked. She'd finished her book and leaked tears over the lovers' tender reconciliation.

She made bread and some light rolls and shared them with old Mrs. Hobbs, who was so fragile Lynn wondered how she managed her slow movements. Her skin was translucent and her frame was so bony that her doctor probably didn't need X rays to examine her.

"Have you been watching 'All My Children'?" Mrs. Hobbs demanded.

"Well, you see, I—" Lynn stumbled.

"I've told you it would help your writing if you'd watch. You should see the new doctor. He likes skinny women!" Mrs. Hobbs did not have her teeth in place, and she lowered her lashless eyelids halfway in a salacious smile.

"It's a good thing he's out of your reach, Mrs. Hobbs. What did your husbands die of? It was exhaustion, wasn't it?"

"That was the second one," Mrs. Hobbs said complacently.

"I can't keep them straight." Lynn grinned. "Why is it that when I whistle you just waggle the drape, but when Bud Turner whistles you wave?"

"I like to brighten his day." Her face wrinkled into a smile.

"He has a perfectly good wife," Lynn reminded her. "And a whole slew of kids."

"No wonder!" She rolled her eyes up.

"Mavis Hobbs, you are a shocking woman," Lynn scolded. "Here you can hardly even get out of bed—"

"I can too get out of bed! I just like to be ready if the opportunity arises..." and she went off into a spasm of choking laughter that scared Lynn spitless.

But Mrs. Hobbs recovered and wiped her eyes with slow laughing sighs and her voice quavered with humor. "I love to see you, Lynn. You are so funny."

"I've put you in a book," Lynn told her. "You're a courtesan."

"Perfect! How'd you think of that?"

"Typecasting." Lynn gave her a smile.

That delighted the old lady. "What's my man like?"

"He's big and he carries you around and makes mad, passionate love to you."

Mrs. Hobbs grinned. "Hot diggity. How?"

"The usual way," Lynn joked. "And you get his secrets."

"'Secrets'? Who wants 'secrets,' you silly child."

"It's important because he's involved in the take-over."

"Oh. Governments." Mrs. Hobbs flipped a scrawny hand. "Phooey. Who cares?"

"You haven't been watching the news."

"No," Mrs. Hobbs admitted. "I figure it's past my time to fret over the world. It's up to the next generation. If I start thinking how people are treating other people, about who is starving or imprisoned or being killed, I can't sleep. So I watch the soaps and I visit my friends on the phone and I leave the whole mess up to the younger bunch."

"You still vote." Lynn's features were soft.

"Ah, yes," Mrs. Hobbs admitted. "Straight Republican."

"How do you know there isn't a rascal among the Republicans?"

Her wrinkles almost smoothed out in her shock. "A Republican rascal?"

"It wouldn't be unheard of."

"Go wash your mouth out with soap!" Mrs. Hobbs exclaimed.

"Now Mavis, you know very well there are good Democrats."

"I resist knowing that," the old lady replied. "When you've learned all the lessons you're supposed to, you die. I've learned all the others—that's the only thing left."

"So that's how it works," Lynn smiled fondly.

Placidly Mrs. Hobbs replied, "Of course."

"Bud Turner is a Democrat."

"What a perfectly dreadful thing to say about such a darling man!" Mrs. Hobbs had a wicked gleam in her eye. "Shame on you."

"You knew!" Lynn was astonished.

"Charity, my child, is one of the things I've already learned."

"As soon as I said there are good Democrats, I thought, 'My God, what have I done?' I thought I was teaching you the last thing you had to learn and you'd just—"

"Pop off," Mrs. Hobbs finished Lynn's sentence. "Not likely. I'm as healthy as a horse." Laughter erupted unbidden from Lynn, and the old lady joined in but fell into another spasm of choking.

When it was over Lynn said anxiously, "You have to quit laughing so hard."

"Then quit being so funny," Mrs. Hobbs advised.

"I'm not funny at all. It's your own humor. You must behave."

Craftily Mrs. Hobbs changed the subject. "Who is that man I've seen going in and out of your place?"

"I wondered when you'd ask."

"I've been waiting for you to confess," Mrs. Hobbs chided.

"'Confess'?" Lynn exclaimed. "'Confess' what?"

"He's married—" Mrs. Hobbs began speculating.

"He is not!" Lynn disclaimed indignantly.

"And you've been overwhelmed by passion. He just has to have you, so he rushes over, when he can, and you fall into frantic embraces and make wild, mindless love. Do you write from experience?"

"I have a vivid imagination and I live alone," Lynn replied.

"But you were married. And there was Mark Blackwood. Oh, Lynn, I beg your pardon. My mind is becoming unreliable. I'd forgotten." In a placating gesture she moved her hand out toward Lynn.

"There is no way you could ever offend me." Lynn took the fragile claw into her own young hand.

"Does it still hurt?" Mrs. Hobbs asked anxiously.

"Now and then."

"I wish that it didn't. He isn't worth it." Mrs. Hobbs said with certainty.

"It was just the shock of being rejected — again."

"What's the saying?" Mrs. Hobbs's voice quavered. "You have to kiss a lot of frogs before you find a prince. They were both frogs."

"If Mark had loved me, I would have learned to sit on a lily pad and catch flies with my tongue."

Mrs. Hobbs eyed Lynn for a minute, then asked, "Do you really believe that, or does the writer in you just like the sound of that marvelous sentence?"

"It was pretty good, wasn't it? But I don't know," Lynn admitted. "It's been á long time. I'm not sure if it was losing Mark or if the pain was centered on my feelings of rejection. When I recall it now, I feel hurt pride more than anything."

"Don't become too attached to grieving," Mrs. Hobbs cautioned. "It can warp your life. It becomes a comfortable shield and you can use it to excuse all sorts of things, like not wanting to make the effort to stay in the mainstream. Or not loving another man. You need to kiss some more frogs."

"All I'd get would be warts." Lynn was disgruntled.

"I was talking to June..." Mavis Hobbs began gently.

"How is June?" Lynn had never met her, but June was someone Mavis often talked about. Lynn felt she knew almost all of these phone friends.

"She knows the Blackwoods." Mrs. Hobbs paused. Then she went on slowly, "Mark is moving back to town."

Lynn sat very still, feeling nothing.

"I thought I should tell you so you wouldn't be surprised." The old lady watched Lynn with concern.

"I am surprised," Lynn said stonily.

"But you're with me to hear of it—not with strangers."

Lynn's voice was thin as she agreed and said, "Thank you."

"Are you all right?"

"It's something looming before me and I dread it...seeing him again."

"There's always something looming in life," Mrs. Hobbs counseled. "Take it as it comes. It gets smaller as it arrives."

"But if you hadn't warned me, I might not have been braced for it. I could have made a fool of myself."

"You never could." Mavis's voice was a gentle quaver.

"You have more confidence in me than I have."

"You're young yet." Mrs. Hobbs comforted her.

"I'm thirty-two."

Mrs. Hobbs cackled. "Ah, to be thirty-two again!"

"Would you really want to be?" Lynn asked with earnest curiosity.

"Five lifetimes wouldn't be enough. It's all been

fascinating. Even the bad times. And I've known such brave ordinary people. Mankind is magnificent. And womankind isn't bad, either," she couldn't resist adding, and she laughed again and choked. Though Lynn was alarmed it didn't bother Mrs. Hobbs. She struggled and recovered, and when Lynn expressed concern the old lady just said, "It's the only exercise I get," and she laughed again.

When Lynn left Mrs. Hobbs's, she idled for a minute to look around the neighborhood. Most of the large old houses had been turned into apartments, and there weren't many people around during the day. They worked or went to school.

There were five watchers, who either worked shifts or worked at home as she did, and there were nine elderly people they helped keep tabs on. They had worked out a schedule that suited everyone.

There were also volunteers who delivered hot meals each noon to those who were housebound, a visiting nurse made regular visits and each shut-in had someone from his church who checked on him during the week. It was a good system.

Thoughtfully Lynn went back to her place and climbed the stairs, wondering if, were she as old as Mrs. Hobbs and couldn't get out, would she manage to be as lighthearted and cheerful?

Lynn thought Mrs. Hobbs's attitude might simply reflect her basic outlook on life. She remembered seeing a PBS special on the children of pioneers in the Southwest. Was it New Mexico? The man and woman interviewed had shared the same life, but their memories were like night and day.

The man said bluntly that pioneer times were hard and bitter. The woman said they'd had such fun with the visiting between families and impromptu square dancing and singing. They'd shared food and work; they'd made do, so it wasn't as if they'd had it easy. And one time the woman's papa had come home with a windup phonograph! It had been so marvelous!

Maybe people make their own happiness, Lynn pondered. Like Ann Landers said, "If life hands you a lemon, make lemonade." Mrs. Hobbs would do that.

But how was Lynn going to handle the lemon of Mark Blackwood's return? How could she make lemonade out of that anguish? How could she survive living in the same town and seeing him again, or running into his blond wife? She couldn't. She would leave town, she decided, knowing she couldn't.

How could she ever leave Fort Wayne? All her family was here, and she loved her neighborhood. Her friends were very kind and proud of her. Could she give up the chance to watch her nieces and nephews grow up? Could she give up the closeness she shared with them? She could not leave. But how could she ever face Mark and make casual conversation? *Oh, God,* she thought bleakly, *help me.*

Then she thought, *how would Mrs. Hobbs handle such a thing?* And Lynn very clearly saw Mrs. Hobbs, young and vibrant, meeting Mark Blackwood... and giving him a sly wink. That was what Mavis Hobbs would do all right. Lynn might not be able to manage a sly wink but she just might be able to scare up an indifferent smile.

That evening Lynn's younger sister Hope called and said, "Hi, sweetie, Mike wants to talk to you."

And Mike promptly dropped the receiver. He finally said, "You okay?"

"My eardrum is shattered," his Aunt Lynn replied.

He appreciated the humor and said, "An' Lynn, am I coming over to your house... your apartment tomorrow?"

"You want to?" she asked.

"Yeah."

Lynn agreed, "Okay."

"She said yes!" Mike yelled that information to his mother.

Hope came back on the phone. "Bless you."

"Life a bit tedious?"

"I believe," Hope replied, "that when I grow up, I'm going to be an old maid."

"Too late," Lynn replied.

"You sound a little down," Hope said intuitively. "Would you rather the monster not come over?"

"No, no," Lynn assured her. "I'll enjoy him."

"You should have your own kids. You're so great with them."

"That's because I can send them home," Lynn teased.

"Uh... Linnie... I heard today... that—"

"Mark Blackwood is coming back," Lynn supplied the rest.

"Whew! I'm glad I didn't have to be the one to tell

you, but I thought if I didn't, and you ran into him.... Is that why you sound...?"

"No," Lynn told her. "This morning I was visiting Mrs. Hobbs. It's only just occurred to me that one of these days she could die on me and I wouldn't see her again."

"She is a love," Hope agreed gently.

"It's her outlook on life that I need to learn," Lynn explained. "And she might not stick around long enough for me to figure out how to see things her way."

"Just because you happened to tangle with two real bastards...."

"Am I a masochist?" Lynn asked musingly.

"I don't believe you enjoy suffering."

"No," Lynn confirmed. "Not even a little. I'll just have to be very careful." In her mind's eye she saw Kevin's dangerous eyelashes. He was a sinfully seductive threat.

"You'll never see him alone," Hope comforted Lynn. "It would always be with other people."

"And the kids are around during the day," Lynn agreed, envisioning Kevin dealing humorously with their chaperonage.

"Yes, but seeing Karen will be difficult."

"'Karen'?" Then Lynn realized her sister was talking about Mark Blackwood, while she had been thinking of Kevin as the threat. "Oh," she said. "'Karen.' I can avoid her easily enough. After the first time there'll be no problem."

"How about coming to supper this Saturday?" Hope invited.

"'This Saturday'?" Lynn hesitated. "That's the day after tomorrow. I may have plans."

"Oh? A date? You could bring him along."

"No. Not that," Lynn hedged. "Just a couple of people."

'It's open. Just us. You can let us know. It's no big deal."

"I appreciate it. And I'll see Mike in the morning about eight-thirty?"

"Yes. And Lynn? Everyone in town is on your side. It will be Mark and Karen who have it rough."

"I hope not," Lynn replied. "I hope everyone has forgotten it."

"They probably have. Act as if you've forgotten."

"Will you tell the rest of the family I'm okay?"

"How did you guess?" her sister asked.

"You're generally the one they elect to do the dirty work."

There was a soft sigh in Lynn's ear. "We all mean well."

"I know you do, darling, and I really appreciate it. But I'd rather not have any in-depth conversations on how I'm managing, if that's all right with everyone."

"I'll pass the word."

AT EIGHT-THIRTY THE NEXT MORNING Lynn opened her apartment door and waved to Hope, who was already vanishing down the stairs. Then she glanced down at Mike. He was going on five, and looked on the world as if it were his particular oyster. His baby chin had the beginnings of stubbornness, he could walk stiff-legged and he had an indulgent attitude toward all women. "You show all the signs of becoming a male chauvinist," Lynn told him.

He gave her a big, pleased smile and replied, "You're neat."

"Neat"? She looked around the untidy apartment and wished Kevin could have heard that.

Mike helped Lynn carry up a load of wood and then busily stacked it in the rack. He joined her in washing the dishes, and he got in her way a whole lot. After lunch he spurned a nap, saying he was too old. Then he settled in the corner of the sofa, put his thumb in his mouth and went to sleep.

Lynn would have vehemently denied watching, but she saw Kevin's car as soon as it drew to the curb. She flew to the bathroom brushed her hair madly, put on lipstick and said to her reflection, "He's here!"

But her reflection replied, "You idiot! How long does it take you to learn your lesson? How much do you have to have dumped on you before you know you're a patsy? You dummy! Calm down!"

As she emerged from the bedroom she spotted Mike, whom she'd momentarily forgotten. Oddly enough, she didn't want him wakened, so she snatched a piece of paper and got it into the doorbell just in time. She allowed two strangled buzzes, then quietly went through the door and down the stairs.

She opened the street door, and though she looked up at Kevin calmly her heart was in her eyes. He smiled down at her from around the sacks of groceries that she hadn't noticed. "Hi. Miss me?" he said, and leaned to kiss her parted lips.

He was back.

6

"IF YOU COULD TAKE the small bag, we wouldn't risk losing all the rest. And oranges bouncing down the stairs could be dangerous."

"Groceries?" Lynn peered into the bag.

"Oh, yes," he assured her.

"You're not moving your groceries in here," she stated.

In a pained voice he replied, "I'm tired of eating mouse rejects—soft, stale crackers and cheese that looks like a dry, Arizona riverbed." By then he had moved around her and was heading up the stairs. Finding the small sack somehow in her arms, she could do nothing but puff up the stairs after him, hissing, "Be quiet, my nephew is asleep on the sofa."

"He'll develop a permanent curvature," Kevin warned. He paused at the door and looked around. "Did the kid straighten up? The place doesn't look half bad."

She shushed him bossily and went ahead of him into the kitchen. "I'll let you store the refrigerated things here until you leave, but that's all."

"You washed the dishes!" He was incredulous.

"Of course I washed the dishes! Who else would do it?"

"Are you trying to pretend you don't need me?" he asked suspiciously.

"Why don't you just leave right now?" she snapped.

"I have to recover from the climb." He put his hand on his muscular chest and slumped against the counter. Then he frowned at her, his lashes lowered, screening his eyes, and his petulant lower lip inspired corruption as he demanded, "Why didn't you call me? I sat around watching my phone for five days."

She knew it had been five and a half days.

"I finally had to come and check on you because I was sure something had to be wrong. How could you go five days without seeing me?"

Silently she replied, *miserably*. But aloud she said, "If you were that concerned, why didn't you call me?"

"And openly admit I was wondering? What sort of a pushover do you think I am? I'm no adolescent, you know. I'm a cool, mature, experienced man. I know women. They're an open book to me. So why didn't you call?"

She compressed her lips, fighting against a grin, and retorted, "Ladies don't idly call men."

"I know that, but you could have thought up some excuse. You could have fooled me. You're a writer." He waited only a second or two, then said, "Come here and kiss me."

"I will not!" But her body shimmered in anticipation.

"You might as well. You're going to have to do it some time."

Her smile crept out, unbidden. He smiled back and said, "You are just beautiful."

She blushed a little and hurried to ask, "Did you write the love scenes in the snakes' cave?"

"No," he dismissed that. "I wrote you letters."

"You did?" She went oddly still. "What sort of letters? Where are they?"

"They were business letters, and I burned them," he replied. "Actually they burned by themselves. Just went up in a puff of smoke all by themselves. Come here and kiss me."

"If I walked over there and kissed you—" she swallowed "—it would seem very forward."

"I'm forward enough for both of us. I'll come over there." He did, and he took her into his arms. His head came slowly down to hers causing the bottom to drop out of her stomach as he kissed her. She curled her hands around his head and kissed him back.

When he raised his mouth a little, she said, "I didn't ask you to kiss me."

"You didn't? Oh." His voice was low and rumbling and a little husky. "Shall I quit?" He smiled.

"Pretty soon," she whispered.

His answering laugh was so deep and intimate that it tickled along her spine like dancing fingers.

He kissed her again, deeper this time. As she relished the feeling of his full, soft lips, the behavior of her susceptible nerve endings grew unbecomingly raucous.

He lifted his mouth much too soon and she was about to protest, but she, too, was out of breath and had to gasp a couple of times before she could speak. The oxygen activated her brain and all its inhibitions, so she freed herself from Kevin's arms and asked, "Have you ever been married?"

"Almost." He watched her intently.

"What happened?" She pretended not to watch him.

"I don't know." He shrugged, not really interested in that subject. "It just fizzled. Why?"

"Uh...." She groped for a reason. "You have all the instincts of a domesticated man." She could hardly tell him she and Mrs. Hobbs had been discussing him.

"'Domesticated' sounds suspiciously like a farm animal," he protested.

"Nothing quite that rugged."

He raised his eyebrows in mock offense. "Before I rip off all my clothes, swing from the chandelier and have my way with you—only to prove I'm rugged, mind you—why do you label me 'domesticated'?"

"You're tidy and you're very grocery conscious," she told him, tallying his traits.

"That hasn't got anything to do with domesticity. It's called the 'instinct for survival,'" he instructed, and then he asked rather crossly, 'What's wrong with being domesticated? Don't you like domesticated men?"

"My— When I was married," she replied coldly, "he white-gloved the apartment just about every day."

He studied her for a minute. "Let me guess. He could inspect and criticize, but he couldn't clean?"

She nodded. "He wrote, 'Dust me,' on the furniture."

His mouth became a bit grim. "He was in school, if I recall, and carried only the average hours, but he didn't work?"

She shook her head.

"But you worked and cleaned the apartment, cooked the meals and did the laundry and the shopping—" he continued.

"No," she corrected. "He bought the groceries. I was not capable of choosing the best."

"Ah." He looked around here and there as he considered her words. "You're still rebelling?"

"That could well be." It surprised her, but it was probably true.

"And he liked long hair?" He reached out and touched her short, dark curls.

"No, that was Mark," she said.

"'Mark'?"

"He left me for a long-haired blonde two years ago—two weeks before the marriage." She lifted her chin.

Kevin was appalled. "He just took off?"

She shrugged in order to seem indifferent. "I got a telegram. They'd eloped."

"How clever of him." His eyes stayed on her and his tone was scornful.

Lynn held his gaze. "He's coming back to live in Fort Wayne."

"Does that bother you?" His voice was concerned, his expression a careful mask.

Again she shrugged. "Everyone will be watching, expecting it to."

"What a fool," he said contemptuously.

She exploded, "I am not!"

"No," Kevin corrected gently. "Not you—him."

She settled down. In a different voice she explained, "She was opposite to me. She was soft and sweet, big eyed, and she hung on his every word."

"That won't last," Kevin scoffed. "To do what she did took a selfish, ruthless woman, not the soft, sweet one she pretended to be."

"I'm not at all domestic," Lynn told him honestly, confessing it. "I'm probably quite masculine."

"Oh?" It was said politely, but Kevin slowly flicked down her body and amusement danced around his mouth. Then he emphatically shook his head, denying her premise. "The way I have it figured, those guys were both spineless, prissy, self-centered—"

"'Prissy'?" That word surprised her.

"It's the best I could come up with. Where's the thesaurus?"

There was a stirring in the living room, the sound of a large, little-boy yawn, then a thud as Mike rolled off the couch. Kevin looked blank, and Lynn reminded him, "My nephew."

Mike paused in the kitchen door and eyed the strange male in a measuring, very masculine way. Since Lynn's introduction was formal, so was Mike's response. He carefully spaced out, "How do you do?"

Lynn found some cookies that were fresh because she'd been sitting with nieces and nephews so much lately. Mike knelt on a chair by the little kitchen table at the window, dunking his cookies in milk and watching the adults silently, deciding whether he would accept the man.

Without thinking about whose groceries they were, or about her earlier edict, Lynn began busily putting away the food. She picked up a jar of pickles the wrong way; it slipped and she grabbed for it. It slammed against the edge of the counter and broke. Her hand was cut at the base of her left thumb, and it bled.

Mike said, "Uh-oh."

Kevin uttered a wordless sound, grabbed her hand and put it under the tap of running water. Lynn looked ruefully at the spilled pickles and the splattered, sticky pickle juice.

Kevin washed the cut, applied pressure and assured her, "It isn't bad."

"I know." She was still looking at the mess.

"It'll be okay," he told her.

"Right. Look at the mess." She meant the pickle juice.

He misunderstood, because he replied, "Cuts like that, where the veins are near the surface, bleed a lot. Those about the face and head, especially, and those on the fingers."

She grinned. "It's nice to have an ex-med student around in an emergency."

"Are you all right?" He bent his head to examine her face. "Not feeling faint?"

"No," she assured him, "I'm fine."

"Uh, I believe," he said slowly, "I believe I should lie down for a minute."

"Kevin?" She realized he'd gone pale. She took his arm and he followed her with faltering steps to the sofa, where he sank down onto the cushions and lay flat. She ran for a warm cloth and brought it back to put on his forehead. She hovered.

Mike stood militantly watching. "What's the matter?"

Kevin gave him a lackluster grin. "Her blood made me a little woozy." Then he closed his eyes again.

Mike climbed up next to Kevin's shoulder and put a protective arm around the top of Kevin's head. He confided, "When mom cut her knee I almost threw up, but I didn't." He was still impressed that he hadn't. "I know just how you feel. It's different if it's men that get hurt."

"Yeah," Kevin said. The two males were in tune.

Lynn was tenderly amused. "It's a good thing you quit med school."

"I didn't really quit. I have *stick-to-it-ness*. I always finish what I begin." He opened one eye and gave her a significant look, then closed it again. "They invited me to resign. My empathetic responses to the patients were making the whole class ill."

She had to smile, and she sat next to him on the sofa, laying her hand on his chest. "Are you okay now?"

"I think I like this attention," he admitted. "You two are like ministering angels."

"I'm no 'angel,'" Mike scoffed. "I was a shepherd at Christmas."

"How did you do?" Kevin glanced his way.

"Terrific," Mike said promptly.

Lynn agreed, "He was."

"Let me see your hand," Kevin asked her softly.

"I don't think so," she demurred.

"I'll be okay now," he promised. "Blood's never bothered me unduly. It was just the shock...that it was yours."

She gave him a quiet look, which he returned and it was she who broke the contact, stood up and said, "Stay there a little longer. I'll go mop up the pickles."

"I'll do that. You should keep that hand dry." He moved to rise, but she put her hand back on his chest. His own immediately covered hers.

"There's a little...uh...'catsup' in the pickle juice," she said.

"Oh."

"You sweet on her?" Mike asked curiously.

Lynn cringed. "Mike!"

But Kevin grinned and asked, "Do you suppose I could be?"

Mike nodded. "You act like it."

Entertained, Kevin settled back and asked, "How's that?"

"Oh—" Mike considered how to explain "—you act silly."

"Mike!" Lynn protested.

"You do, too," he informed her.

"I'm going to clean up the pickle juice." She turned away.

Mike hopped down from the sofa. "I'll help. *Catsup* doesn't bother me, unless it's my mom's." He shared a grin with Kevin.

Knowing how vigorously Mike would help, Lynn suggested, "Maybe you should stay here and see if Kevin needs any help."

"Oh. Do you want me to?"

"Please."

"Sure." He hopped back up on the sofa and leaned an elbow into Kevin's middle. "You okay?" he asked his charge as Lynn went into the kitchen.

Kevin nodded, then said, "I think you're right. I could very well be a little sweet on her."

"Yeah, I thought so."

"You speak very well for four."

"I'm almost five. Mom says I'm going to be a lawyer." He looked complacent. "I argue a lot. Do you have nephews?"

"No, not even one. I don't have any brothers or sisters."

"Just you?" Mike was surprised.

"Yes. Just me."

"Aw."

"But I have one hundred eighty-seven cousins," Kevin offered.

"That's a lot?"

Kevin nodded. "But all their kids are just cousins, too. I'll just have to marry someone with nieces and nephews to share with me."

"An' Lynn has a bunch," Mike reflected. "And she shares very well."

"Does she?"

"Yeah—like cookies and kisses." He thought about it and added, "I pretend not to like kisses, being a boy. Do you?"

"No. When you're older you appreciate any you can get."

Lynn knew Kevin knew she could hear their conversation.

"I guess that's right," Mike decided. "Dad follows mom around and pesters her to kiss him."

"Does he?" Kevin kept his face smooth and interested.

"And he makes her sit on his lap, and he tickles her."

"And does she like it?" Kevin inquired.

"She pretends not to," Mike confided. "Like me and kissing."

"But she does like it?"

"Yeah." Mike thought that was funny. "She giggles and says, 'Oh, Bobby, you stop that!' His name's Bob, but she calls him 'Bobby' when he tickles her."

Kevin let out a choked cough, and in the kitchen Lynn had to smother giggles. Mike went on freely telling all the family secrets. He told where they hid their extra cash, that mom had to take a laxative just yesterday, that dad liked to sleep in the middle of the bed on top of mom and—

Lynn hurried to the kitchen door and interrupted, "Mike, I don't believe you finished your cookies."

"Is all the *catsup* gone?" He grinned at Kevin, sharing the joke, as he slid off the couch. Then he reached up and ran a companionable hand along Lynn's hip as she passed him coming out of the kitchen.

Lynn looked down on a comfortably supine Kevin. "Well, you've learned just about everything."

"Do you giggle when you're tickled?"

"I'm a stoic." She met his gaze blandly.

He grinned before he asked, "How's the hand?"

"No problem."

"That thumb may not want to be jostled for a day or two," he cautioned.

"Yeah," she agreed, then asked in turn, "How are you doing?"

"I'll be here the rest of my life. Who could pry themselves free of this god-awful sofa?"

"You're really not very kind about that sofa."

"Why did you ever buy it?" He sounded as if he'd already gnawed on that question.

"It was left here."

"That's understandable. It was probably abandoned at the first opportunity. If you kissed me, it might give me the strength to...get up." He smiled slyly.

"What about Mike?" She looked down her nose at him. "He'll go home and blab that you kissed me, and the whole family will think I'm carrying on with a man."

"I could move in," he offered helpfully. "That would really get them excited."

She became serious. "There is no way I'm going to get tangled up with another man. And I work alone."

"I really wasn't thinking of working. And I'm not just any ordinary man."

She conceded his last point. "You were considering hanky-panky, right?"

"Something more on that order. Then when I give you the kiss of forgetfulness you'd really have something to forget and I wouldn't be needlessly expending energy. Those forgetfulness kisses are depleting."

"The effort is probably expended before the kiss is necessary," she countered.

He smiled as he considered her angle, then her angles. "Let's go argue about who will sleep in the middle of the bed the way Mike's parents do."

"No. You are shocking."

"And you'd love my connections. Let's go mix it up." He leered at her and she grinned. Her lips were parted to reply, when Mike came back into the living room, wiping his mouth on his sleeve. Lynn started to stand up, but Kevin took her arm and asked urgently, "What were you going to say?"

"That the only thing that's going to get mixed up is a cake."

"You wretch!" He reached up and swatted her bottom. She squeaked and jumped away.

Mike sighed heavily and shook his head. "Just like mom and dad."

Lynn immediately snapped, "No!" But Kevin laughed.

So THE NEXT DAY, when Hope called her and mentioned a list of mundane things, obviously to lull her into a placid, unsuspecting state, Lynn said she was very busy and managed to hang up. She immediately realized that hadn't been the smart thing to do. Mike had talked, her sister was curious and Lynn should have tackled the subject and killed off the speculation, because anything that festered grew.

Two days later her brother called and said, "I understand there's a new man in your life. I'm sure glad, what with Mark Blackwood coming back to town."

Lynn knew the whole family had been discussing Mike's report, so she asked, "'New man'? What 'new man'?"

"Mike said there was a guy there, and he fainted when you cut your hand and had to lie on the sofa, and he patted your bottom."

At least Mike was reasonably accurate. "I am collaborating on a book with Kevin Walker," she stated formally.

"'Kevin Walker'? The sci-fi writer?"

"Yes," she replied shortly.

"Hey, he's terrific! I'd like to meet him." He turned from the phone and told someone else, "It's Kevin Walker...." Then he must have been hushed, because he came right back on the phone and, searching for conversation, blurted, "How's your hand?" Obviously he'd been prompted.

"Who's there with you?" Lynn demanded.

"Uh...who's here?" He paused for instructions. "Who's here with me?" Stalling, he waited to be told what to reply. He simply was not cut out for intrigue.

Through her teeth Lynn said, "Yes. Who—is—there—with—you?"

"Oh. Here? Well...just...Jerry!"

A blatant lie. It was more than likely her mother who had made her brother call, and he was doing such a lousy screen job he would probably not be asked again. Doubtless her mother was right there next to him. "Why isn't Jerry at work?" Lynn asked.

"Oh. 'Why isn't Jerry at work....' Jerry, why aren't you at work?" He paused, then said into the phone, "He doesn't feel well."

"Well, you can tell *Jerry* that there is nothing between Kevin Walker and me." With that she hung up.

No one in the family asked her any more direct questions. They asked a whole lot of roundabout questions, leading questions and implied questions, but there were no more direct ones. Lynn found herself explaining briskly that she was collaborating on a book, that it was a professional opportunity instigated by their mutual agent, and that was all!

But was it? She had begun to dream about Kevin. And the dreams didn't involve social occasions with polite conversation and handshaking. Oh, no. They were steamy, erotic encounters that got worse. Better. Ecstatic. She'd waken in the night with the covers all askew and her nightgown twisted and wrapped around her so tightly that she looked like she was part rope.

And she'd lie awake, reminding herself of what

crippling episodes two men had already brought to her life. Both those relationships had begun with humor and attraction, too. She would be a fool to trust another man.

7

IT TOOK ANOTHER DAY or so before Lynn really faced
the problem of Kevin Walker. She decided any man
that physically attractive had to have flaws. No one
was perfect. And since Kevin was flawless in face
and form, his would have to be flaws of character.

He was an only child. He was probably spoiled
rotten and completely self-centered. And at almost
thirty years of age, he lived with his parents. That
was unusual. Of course, he was conserving money
as he made the transition to full-time writing, but it
was something to think about. He could be very de-
pendent.

Their acquaintanceship had been under rather re-
stricted circumstances. There had been no one to
distract him from her. He had set out deliberately to
charm her, and he'd done that easily enough. No
doubt he was practiced, since he was assuredly very
attractive and likable. Her only protection against
him depended on sorting him out. She needed only
to unmask him—expose his flaws—and she would
be disillusioned.

Now how was she supposed to do that?

Her mother had always told her and her sisters
that to choose a man one should use simple guide-

lines. He would be a man you could respect; one who had friends; a man other women liked but to whom he responded casually, in a friendly though not flirtatious manner. He wouldn't be too fond of gambling or drinking. He would laugh with you and not at you. He would talk and listen in turn, and he would be a man who not only wanted to make love to you but would care for you and cherish you.

All those things were a helpful gauge. She could measure Kevin against the list and see how he fared. She'd never really studied Steve or Mark. She'd been blind to their flaws. If she'd just paid attention she would have saved herself a lot of grief. There had to have been all sorts of indications of Steve's selfishness if she had wanted to see them.

And Mark. She'd been so entranced after meeting him, so ready to finally love again, that she'd kept him to herself. They'd met Karen quite by accident and then seemed to stumble over her at every turn. Of course, Mark was susceptible and had allowed Karen to lure him away from her. He was stolen before she knew what had happened.

Her mother's guidelines could reveal a wealth of discredits in a man. With so many possibilities, Lynn hardly knew where to begin with Kevin. But she was deluding herself. She knew exactly where she'd start. She would see if Kevin was susceptible to other women. There was no need to fool around with the lesser flaws. For such a test, Lynn deliberately chose Betina.

Exactly how she was going to get Kevin and Betina together was something of a problem. He might misunderstand if Lynn suddenly invited him out when she professed that their relationship was strictly a business one. Lynn pondered the problem and waited for an opportunity to arrange a meeting.

The days passed, with Kevin and Lynn working steadily on the book at her apartment. Kevin brought over groceries, stocked the shelves and cooked their meals as if it were a completely natural and ordinary thing to do. And he refused to let her reimburse him for the food when she offered.

"I told you if you furnished the place, I'd provide the meals," he reminded her.

In a flash of brilliance Lynn decided she would take him out to eat, thereby paying off her obligation to him and, more important, setting things up for another "repayment," which would include Betina.

Lynn watched Kevin, who had gone back to work. He was lounging on the sofa, his shoes off, his hair messed up, and he was chewing on his pencil as he read through a rough chapter.

Relaxed, he reminded her of a warrior who was home and at ease. His body was marvelous. It was her interest in the human figure as an art form that made her so conscious of him. It was her art appreciation that made her so intrigued by his body. Yeah. Sure.

"Do you swim?" She could see his body in the water....

"Yes." He glanced up. "Why?"

She had said it aloud! "Uh...would you like to go swimming?" Her errant tongue came readily to her rescue and she listened to her invitation with some amazement. Of course it would serve—Club O had a superb restaurant, plus an indoor heated pool.

"Do you plan to go down to the river, break the ice and paddle around?" Kevin smiled easily at her.

"No," she replied a bit haughtily. "I belong to Club O. We could swim Sunday morning and have brunch there. I'd like to return the favor of your cooking, but I don't dare fix a meal for you—you'd be too disappointed."

"I don't know about that. Your bread beats anything I've ever tasted."

Lynn tried to accept that without a beam of satisfaction, but her smile crept out. "You'll go?" That had been almost too easy.

"I'd be delighted."

It was her first step to becoming disillusioned with him and freed of her bemusement. She made the reservations, and on the next Sunday Kevin picked her up at the apartment and they drove to Club O in his red car.

Lynn thought how nice it was to belong to a swim club so that in the middle of winter you could take a man swimming and see how well-coordinated he was.

Now be honest, Lynn, she said to herself. *What you actually want to see is if he's really as well made as he seems. Right? There's always the chance he'll be knock-kneed or bowlegged or have a paunch. True.*

But, then, what worked one way—her seeing him almost entirely stripped down—worked the other way, too. She would in turn be very exposed to his eyes. It did work out that way.

Lynn had resisted the low-cut, high-cut, cut-out scarlet Speedo she had once bought on impulse. Who would ever have the nerve to wear it, anyway? But she had been tempted to try it that day.

Instead she wore her old, no-nonsense, practice Speedo with its equally high-scooped front and back. With her wearing that, Kevin couldn't get any mistaken idea that she was trying to show off for him.

She was the only woman at Club O that day in a practice Speedo.

Kevin left the men's locker room and walked out to the Olympic-size heated pool. He stood facing a three-sided, two-story bank of glass that looked out on winter. It was a strange feeling to be surrounded by lush plants, about to go swimming, at this time of year. He looked around for Lynn.

She was in the pool, submerged up to her nose. He grinned at her, walked over, dived effortlessly into the pool and swam underwater. He came up in front of her and surfaced, facing her. Droplets beaded his skin, his hair and his eyelashes in a very attractive way.

"The food here is just terrific," she said in a nervous burst. "The chefs win all the awards right across the board. You're in for a treat."

"I'm looking forward to it." He swam in a lazy circle around her, and the water glistened on his muscular shoulders. Lynn was unaccountably nervous and was relieved when he said, "Come on, let's swim."

She struck out smoothly and they swam to one end and back, repeating the length until they were warm in the heated pool. They moved with leisurely strokes, and Kevin began to talk to her. "Have you belonged to this club for very long?" He was amused by his own formality, but Lynn was acting as though it were the first time they'd met.

"Almost half my life. My folks think swimming is important."

"You swim very well," he complimented her.

"Thank you." What an idiotic conversation, Lynn railed at herself. She wanted to say he wasn't knock-kneed, after all, and she thought he should model at the art school, but she hated the idea of the female students leering at him. He would sit there in his muscles and a jock strap and nothing else—not even a blush. He was very comfortable with himself, and he was not the least bit self-conscious. Not like her.

"You're sleek and lovely." He grinned as he said that to her.

"In my Speedo practice suit." Now what made her stupid tongue blurt that out as if she were embarrassed about wearing it?

"It's very attractive."

She gave him an exasperated look.

"It's like a second skin. Oh, to be some silky cloth and get to cling to you."

"Don't be silly," she scolded primly, but she blushed with pleasure.

They swam and then strolled around so he could snoop into the saunas and exercise rooms, and they sat on the edge of the hot whirlpool. She watched the women there watching Kevin. He did not appear to notice them. He watched her. And his attention to her made it very difficult for her to stare at him as she wanted to, ogle him as she desired.

She "desired"? How strange that particular word should come to her mind. It was not that she "desired" him, it was just that he was so attractive. It was normal to appreciate well-made things. That is, well-made men. And he was very well made. Actually, he was awesome.

Did any other man have that particular, fascinating pattern of chest hair that tapered so enticingly to his navel in a sleek ridge? It was almost like an arrow. Then, again, the pattern might not be an arrow down as much as it might be a surging growth upward from... from that nest of potency bulging there. An atomic burst of male virility. She took a breath and her eyes almost crossed.

Kevin watched in amusement as Lynn twitched slightly and blushed. What was she thinking? Sitting there in her practice Speedo, her tempting body curled modestly on the edge of the whirlpool, she appeared never to look directly at him. But he knew that she did.

Why should she be so awkward with him? She was like a high-school girl on her first date—tongue-tied, tense, self-conscious—and his heart was touched.

"We probably should go get dressed," Lynn broke into his thoughts. "At least I should. I have to dry my hair or I look like a water witch."

"You have ducktails." He lifted a finger and touched her head here and there, and she was astonished that the roots of her hair extended all the way to her breasts and down farther to the core of her body. It was amazing that his touching her hair made her tingle in those distant roots.

She rose in a trance, distantly aware that in a lithe, effortless movement Kevin did, too. He walked her to the entrance of the women's locker room, and she mumbled, "I'll see you at the desk." And she noted that he nodded with a tender sort of smile.

As she dressed she scolded herself for being a klutz. They always debated and argued, and yet today she couldn't string two words together. This sudden awkwardness was stupid. Just because it was almost as if they were on a date she wasn't comfortable with him. That had to be his fault. He was acting dumb. He was being so amused. It was probably the Speedo. He thought she looked silly and it embarrassed him to be seen with her.

Then why had he stayed so close? He could have said he liked swimming and just gone off. Or diving. He was a great diver. Or he could have escaped into the sauna. Or talked to the eager women who were trying to attract his attention. But, no, he hadn't moved from her side. Good manners. He had been raised to behave correctly.

What on earth would they talk about over brunch? What was happening in the world? What interested him? She interested him. He had made that clear enough. But she could hardly start a conversation with: "What is it about me that interests you?" She knew darned well what interested him—an affair.

She stood in front of the bank of mirrors, gazing into them, drying her hair, but she didn't see herself reflected there; she saw Kevin. That troubled her, for Kevin made her think of sex.

"They" said that while men's sexual appetites peaked at the age of seventeen, women hit their full sexual drive at thirty-five. She could well be dealing with that problem. She was being driven by her biological clock, therefore she found Kevin attractive—damned near irresistible.

Into her mind came a picture of her ravening after Kevin, and his fleeing in terror. But she didn't believe he'd flee. Not right away. He might if he found out her sex drive was a little higher than average. Steve had complained.

So... what would they talk about as they selected from the stunning array of artistically arranged, succulent foods? Well, they could talk about how the food looked. Then at the table they could comment on how it tasted. How thrilling.

It was with an odd reluctance that she packed her suit, towel and hair dryer into her kit and with a thrill of anticipation went out to Kevin. How could she be reluctant and anticipating at the same time? It had to be hormones.

She met Kevin in the health-club lobby, and they went up the carpeted, mirrored stairs to the elegant restaurant. As they were being led to their table, they were intercepted by two of Lynn's male friends. In a confusion of greetings they said, "Lynn! Hi! Is it just the two of you? Great. Come sit with us." They looked with curiosity at Kevin as they hustled the couple over to a long table. There they were cheerfully greeted by the others, who rose and shifted and included the arriving couple into the group almost as if they were being absorbed.

There were four other men and three women. At first they were a little formal with Kevin, but he was perfect—seeing to it that Lynn was seated, firm he was not going to sit across the table but next to her; and he shook hands and replied to the others with easy charm.

Lynn did not want to sit with a crowd. She had not come to Club O with Kevin in order to sit with a bunch of hooligans. While this was going through her mind, all the others were acting normal, cheerful, friendly, talking a blue streak and laughing. She was a quiet puddle of sulk.

Kevin was a part of the whole and there was so much conversation and laughter and ribbing going on that they didn't need a sparkling Lynn to help out.

Of course, it being February in Indiana, there was only one subject; basketball. At their table everyone was well versed in which Indiana high schools generally had what sort of teams, and they kept track of how each team was faring.

They proceeded to make bets on the coming state championships, the college basketball winners, and then they went on to discuss the professional teams. They guessed game-point spreads, wrote down all the bets and arranged a payoff dinner when the season was finished. And Kevin was right in the thick of it all.

They spent three hours eating, arguing, laughing, talking, eating more and agreeing, debating, convulsing with guffaws and eating even more. The staff was very patient though their group was one of the last to finally leave the club.

One of Lynn's friends said, "We'll get together soon," and another exclaimed, "Lynn, where did you find him?" That was one of the women, naturally. "This has been great. We'll do it next Sunday."

"We'll see," Lynn hedged. If she and Kevin started meeting with groups of her friends, they would become a "couple," and she didn't want that. This was a business partnership between Kevin and her. She did not want it turning into regular social meetings or dating, and besides, this was only part of her plan.

As Kevin drove her home, he smiled at her and said, "I enjoyed being with your friends." His eyes had gone back to the road.

She replied with a noncommittal, "Um." Then on its own her tongue added, "You fitted in well."

"They all love you and I rode in on their affection for you." He came to a red light and stopped in the line of traffic before he glanced at her in a penetrating way to ask, "Did you ever date any of them?"

"No."

That appeared to surprise him. He shifted gears as the light changed to green, and the car moved, taking his attention, but he asked, "Why not?"

"I wasn't interested."

That made him smile.

She waited a while and then asked, "How much did you bet?"

"Altogether about...oh, about twenty dollars." He gave her a quick friendly glance.

"It sounded as if you were all betting your shirts."

"No. Gambling is fun now and then, but when it's serious betting it isn't for me. This wouldn't apply under all circumstances, because the term 'gambling' has other ramifications. For instance, I'm gambling right now on being able to fully support myself with writing. I find that particular gamble exciting and I have a large stake in winning."

"You're a very talented writer."

"I return the compliment." His tone was serious and her little smile came back.

THEY WORKED HARD that week. It had come about quite naturally that as they worked together they jogged together, too. Kevin kept a sweat suit in the trunk of his car, but he used Lynn's shower. That seemed very intimate to her, and she would think of him naked in her bath and shivers would run inside her body.

Inevitably, Kevin met Mrs. Hobbs. Once, as Lynn whistled and waited for the drape to waggle, she had told Kevin, "If she realized a man was down here with me, she'd wave, instead of just waggling the drape."

It didn't take Mavis Hobbs long to realize Lynn was jogging with a gorgeous man, and she demanded Lynn introduce him to her. As they walked over through the icy February day, Lynn warned, "She's a dreadful flirt."

"I wish you were a flirt."

"I wouldn't know how." She smiled a little as she

watched the toes of her boots walking along the frozen ground.

"Of course not," he said with humor in his voice.

She looked up at him, surprised by his tone, but his eyelashes hid his expression like a mask.

In her bed Mrs. Hobbs lay against piled pillows, wearing a lacy bed jacket with a high lace ruffle around her throat. The old lady had once told Lynn that high collars hid the lines on her neck caused by losing weight, and she had laughed. She indicated it wasn't age that lined her face and throat; it was weight loss.

Being an ex-med student, Kevin had obviously taken Bedside Manners I and II, for he sat on the side of Mrs. Hobbs's bed and took her frail, transparent, bony little hand between his strong, warm hands, and he said, "You look very comfortable."

So naturally Mrs. Hobbs flipped back the edge of the comforter and suggested, "Would you like to join me?"

Kevin loved it and replied, "You're a naughty lady."

And Mavis Hobbs agreed.

The old lady was very animated and saucy, but when she laughed and choked Lynn was alarmed. Kevin was there, though, taking Mrs. Hobbs in his big hands and gently turning her so she could breathe. His face was watchful, serious and very kind.

After they had settled her again and were sure she was all right, they returned through the icy wind to Lynn's apartment. Lynn sneezed at the same time that Kevin coughed. They laughed, but then she sneezed again and he looked closely at her.

Back at the apartment Lynn continued to sneeze and felt as if she'd walked through a door labeled Full-blown Cold. She took vitamin C and drank orange juice. Then she began to shiver. It was soon apparent she had more than a simple cold.

"Go take a hot shower," Kevin ordered. "Stand in it until you're really warm."

"I hope I didn't leave any stray germs with Mrs. Hobbs."

"You weren't near her," Kevin reminded her. "Go get in the shower."

Lynn was drying off and started when the bath door opened a crack—enough for Kevin's arm to reach inside. A clean sweat suit dropped from his hands onto the floor by the door and his voice instructed, "Put that on."

He had been through her drawers? Good Lord! She put the suit on. Old and soft, it was extremely comfortable, but not very flattering. She fretted.

He watched her emerge from the bath. The way the sweat suit gently molded her lovely body was mind-boggling. He drew in a quick breath, but disciplined himself to lean over and pull back the down comforter and sheet. She was obviously embarrassed.

In the bed he'd placed a bleach bottle filled with hot water and wrapped in a T-shirt. "That's the only thing I could find to use as a hot-water bottle," he explained.

Lynn crawled into bed and curled around the hot

bottle and went to sleep. The sound of clinking glass woke her and eyes opened on an evening-darkened room. Kevin was maneuvering a tray to her bedside.

"What time is it?" She croaked like a frog.

"Suppertime. I've made you some hot broth. Can you sit up? Would you like to wash your face?" His voice was gravelly.

She returned from the bathroom shivering and rolled back into bed. Kevin came from the kitchen, having replaced the hot water in the bleach bottle.

She wasn't hungry. He coaxed, "Drink the soup." And he watched her do it.

It did help her throat, and she curled back down to sleep again.

She wakened in the dark and tried to figure out what was going on. She needed to gargle. She hated to get out of bed, because the room was cool and her body did not want to cope with cool air. She stirred and coughed, and Kevin came in from the living room. "How are you doing?" He seemed to have a foggy voice.

Her own sounded like a robot reject. "What are you doing here?"

"It's early yet," he soothed. "I thought I'd get you settled for the night and then I'd sleep on the sofa."

"No!" she quacked. "You can't spend the night! My neighbors would all know."

"But you need me." He was insistent. "You're sick."

"I'll survive." She struggled with the words. "Go home."

"You need me." He was adamant.

"Go home!" she begged ardently. "You must!"

"That's ridiculous."

"I can't help it. I didn't invent the manners and mores. Go home." She was dizzy. She would go back to sleep. He would stay. Everyone would know. "Promise me you'll go home."

'Okay, okay," he grumbled. "But I'll be here in the morning."

SHE WAS DELIRIOUS. She struggled to do something with all her might. She wanted something. It was just beyond reach. If she tried just a little harder, she could make it. She opened her eyes as she reached... and Kevin was there in the daylight.

"Kevin?" she questioned in a voice full of wonder.

"Hello. Are you okay? Here, take these." He held a glass to her lips. "Swallow a little water first— they'll go down easier."

"What are they?" She managed the words.

"One is an antibiotic," he explained softly. "With such a bad throat and the fever, you need a little help. The others will clear your head and ease the pain in your throat."

"How did you get the medication?" She swallowed the pills painfully past her wickedly sore throat.

"One of the doctors here in Fort Wayne is an old classmate of mine who went on to graduate. I gave him your symptoms and he gave me the prescription." His voice was husky.

"Doctors never give prescriptions until they see the patient." She was sure.

"He trusted my diagnosis." Kevin tipped up the glass to indicate she was to drink it all.

"It hurts to swallow," she complained pitiably.

"I know." He smoothed her hair back from her forehead in a particularly comforting way. "After breakfast there are a couple more pills you have to take, but you need some food in your stomach for them to sit on."

"Yeah." She was already sinking into lethargy. She dozed. She heard the phone and the rumble of his voice and in a while he coaxed her into eating some Cream of Wheat with brown sugar. She docilely allowed him to feed her, though she did wonder vaguely where he had got Cream of Wheat.

During the day he gave her hot liquid Jell-O to sip past her sore throat and 7UP, and later on he fed her slivered fresh strawberries, sugared and juicy. "They're from Africa," he told her, but she just said, "Um."

He fed her hot beef broth that was unseasoned, and he fed her sliced bananas in cream. It seemed to her that the whole day he kept waking her to drink something or take pills or eat something. And he used a warm cloth wrung almost dry to freshen her face and hands. It was lovely.

The variety of foods did penetrate, and she finally gave up trying to remember if she'd had any of those in her kitchen. She understood he'd bought it all and she must owe him another brunch.

She ate and drank obediently, gargled when she went to the bathroom and downed what seemed like an endless parade of pills. Each day she showered, put on another sweat suit and went back to a bed that Kevin had stripped and made up fresh.

It was on the fourth day that she bothered to look into the bathroom mirror and she was appalled. Her hair resembled a tired wig that had lain for some time unnoticed on a garage floor. And she didn't recognize the soft sherry-colored jogging suit she was wearing.

As she again lay against the pillows in the freshly made up bed, she asked vaguely, "Where did I get the jogging suit?"

"It does match your eyes." He was pleased.

"You bought it?" she croaked.

"Um. Open your mouth." His voice was husky and rough.

"Have you caught my sore throat?"

"No, no. Just empathy. Open your mouth."

"I could feed myself." Actually, she loved having him feed her, but it seemed so...personal.

He ignored her feeble protest as he offered another spoonful.

"Have you been home?" she queried.

"Just the way you said."

"It's been several days." Her eyes were big as she looked up at him.

He smiled and made a sound of agreement.

"Did anyone call me?"

"Whom did you expect?" He was cautious.

"Well...my family? They generally keep close tabs."

"I told them you had laryngitis. A couple of other people, too."

"I see." She opened her mouth for another bite of oatmeal...oatmeal? "You've been very kind." How inadequate.

"You needed me." He smiled. "Your temperature is down." His voice was so tender. "You need to stay in bed another day or so, but we nearly have this licked."

"I'm impressed."

"It's been my pleasure."

IN ANOTHER DAY she was even more lucid and felt much better. She had slept too long, though, and she was restless. When Kevin came into the room she was so aware of him as a desirable man that her senses almost went berserk.

Lynn was reasonably discreet about it, but her breath needed monitoring, her tongue restlessly licked along her lip and her eyes didn't know where to look. "It's time for me to get up," she said very, very earnestly.

"How about tomorrow?" He offered as he set a tray on her bedside table. It held a glass of pineapple juice and some of the inevitable pills.

"How about now...for a little while?" She made her voice as urgent as she could and blinked so her eyes would not languidly trail down his body.

"Let's see how frisky you are after your bath."

"Frisky"? That was most of her trouble.

"If you promise to dry your hair thoroughly this morning before you leave the warm bathroom, you may wash it." He gave the permission generously.

She had planned to, anyway. It was driving her

wild, it was so dirty. She hadn't washed it for days, however long it had been, and it felt as if she'd used solid lard on it as a hair dressing. With it the way it was, if God leaned down from heaven to give her a blessing, His hand would slide right off her head.

Kevin lay something yellow and towellike on the end of the bed and told her, "When you dress, put this on."

"What is that?" She stared at the soft yellow whatever-it-was. "You didn't buy me something else, did you?"

"I'm deducting it from the royalties from our book."

Her stare went to him. "But that'll be a long time...a year or more."

"You're good for it. I'll trust you."

As she crawled out of bed, she noticed she was wearing the streaked and faded purple sweat suit. "I love the cinnamon one," she said to Kevin.

"Sherry," he corrected. "It matches your eyes."

The bath zapped her. She was not quite as frisky when she emerged clean and scrubbed in the new yellow jogging suit. She was still sick enough that she needed the heavier garment in bed so she didn't feel chilled. She felt a little light-headed and decided it was because her hair was so clean.

Her bed had been stripped and remade, but the down comforter was missing. She went to the door of her bedroom and looked into the living room. Kevin was just making a nest for her on the sofa. There was a cozy fire in her fireplace, and there was a pot of tea with two cups on a tray on the drop-leaf table.

Kevin glanced up and paused. "My God, you look gorgeous!"

She pretended nonchalance and replied, "It does make a difference when one's hair isn't slicked down with grease."

He raised his eyes to her fluffy riot of short hair and noticed it, then went back to her eyes, which had taken on some yellow lights from the jogging suit. And then he had to look down her body.

The suit was soft and loving on her. He watched her body as it moved inside it when she sat down on the nest he'd made for her. It made him glad that she wore his gift, and he felt great contentment that he was the one who had taken care of her and made her well.

Covertly Lynn studied Kevin. He was too attractive. She really needed to discover his defects. She sneaked little peeks at him as she blushed and tried to appear casual about being in the same room with him.

She had to see him with Betina. And as soon as she was well enough she would. But in the meantime she would be stiff and aloof around him— purely in the interest of self-preservation.

IT WAS A WEEK before Lynn forced herself to phone Betina. How strange that she seemed reluctant to make the call. Of course, she had avoided Betina for two whole years, with good reason.

Betina was a dreadful flirt. She was also tall, shapely, delightful fun, and she had long, blond hair. She was a lot like Karen. Grimly Lynn dialed her number.

"Lynn!" Betina exclaimed with a delighted laugh.

"How've you been?" Lynn observed the standard social ritual before she arranged for the meeting between Betina and the undoubtedly flawed Kevin.

"We've not been together in an age!" Betina bubbled impatiently. "Why not get together this Friday? Shall I find someone for you?" She meant that kindly, and Lynn knew it. Betina's circle of friends included every eligible male within a hundred-mile radius of Fort Wayne. She could make a fortune as a dating bureau.

"Thanks," Lynn said. "I'll bring someone I've just met. He's a writer and rather interesting."

"Oh?" Betina was intrigued. "Anything serious?"

"Of course not." Oddly Lynn could not exhale. She had just deliberately thrown Kevin to the wolves as if he were fresh bait. Why should that affect her so terribly? She forced herself to take deep, slow breaths, and after she hung up Lynn went out and jogged.

When Kevin came to her house that day, she invited brusquely, "Would you like to go out to dinner on Friday?"

He almost gasped as his head came up sharply to look at her. "Why, Lynn, I'd love to. How nice."

And then she explained awkwardly, "I appreciate all you did when I was sick."

As Friday approached, Lynn was confounded by how much she was dreading the evening. Her head hurt so badly that she almost called dinner off. It was a classic tension headache; all her muscles were knotted and her teeth were tightly clenched. How stupid. What did she care?

Then she had to struggle with the impulse to wear a slinky, plunging-necklined, spangled, disgracefully wicked wisp. She'd worn it once over long underwear to a Fine Arts Ball, as a joke.

But why in the world would she try to compete with Betina? The whole purpose of this fiasco was to prove he was susceptible. Why try to prevent knowing? Besides, theirs was a business relationship, and she was beginning to think it was really silly that she would go to all this trouble to discover his flaws. His character was of no concern to her.

She finally faced the fact that she was loath for Kevin to meet Betina. And she analyzed that reaction. She decided it was because Kevin would be mesmerized by Betina and Lynn would be bored stiff with nothing to do all evening. It wasn't just that Kevin was going to meet Betina; she hated the thought of having a boring evening.

Kevin came for her Friday night and he was so handsome in his blue suit, white shirt and maroon tie that she almost changed out of the high-necked, long-sleeved, blue silk shirtwaist into that spangly, wicked wisp without the long underwear. It showed character that she did not.

Lynn had arranged to meet Betina and her date Marvin at Casaburo's for an Italian dinner. After that they would go dancing. Kevin would dance with Betina.

It would be only good manners for the couples to

trade partners and dance. Kevin would hold Betina in his strong arms and against his hard body— Betina always danced as if she were glued to a man. It was a miracle Lynn's teeth didn't shatter at the very thought; her jaws tried hard enough in the attempt.

As they drove up Clinton toward Casaburo's Lynn decided she needed to go out more. If going on a date made her this tense, then she certainly needed to go out more. She spent the rest of the way running over all the men she knew, and rejected every one.

As Lynn had anticipated, Betina wore a shocking gown. Lynn took one look at her and then watched for Kevin's predictable reaction. His eyes took in Betina. Then they slid to Lynn's, and he grinned at her to share the humor. After that he looked only at Betina's face.

Their conduct at dinner was reasonable. The food was perfect, the service excellent and the conversation easy enough. Gradually Lynn noticed that Betina, effervescent as ever, was flirting as usual, but only with her date! Her attitude toward Kevin was friendly, but the attention she lavished on her own date was enough to put him on the rafters. The man was only amused.

Kevin and Marvin kept the conversation general. Marvin distracted Betina from himself and made her include the others in the conversation, while Kevin encouraged a tongue-tied Lynn to respond.

It was a weird evening for Lynn. She'd expected to be left isolated as both men ignored her and fawned over Betina.

That had happened several times when she had been with Betina. But since it wasn't happening this time, Lynn wasn't exactly sure how to act. She was that astounded.

After the two couples left Casaburo's and had gone on to several other places to dance, they did switch partners. Marvin danced with Lynn and he talked easily to her, apparently unaware of her monosyllabic replies as she stared piercingly at Betina and Kevin, who were also dancing.

Kevin held Betina loosely as they laughed and chatted—perfectly normal. Betina was behaving just like any normal female. Lynn had never realized Betina was capable of "normal."

And Kevin danced with Lynn. He didn't dance with her the way he danced with Betina. He pulled her close and held her against his strong body. He put his mouth against her temple, and it was just fabulous!

He didn't chat her up or laugh or make jokes. He breathed his hot breath into her hair and he kissed along her temple. His big hand on her back burned through her shirtwaist, and he moved his hand slightly, as if he were resisting moving it a whole lot more.

"I love the feel of you through that silk," he groaned against her forehead. And his arm muscles under her hand were tensed and bunched just as hers were. Maybe he didn't date much, either. How preposterous! He probably had to fend off women.

When they returned to their table, Kevin seated her and then pulled his chair close to hers. Lynn was so engrossed in confused thoughts whirling in her brain that she wasn't paying much attention to what was going on.

An old friend, Pete, came over to say hello. He knew both her and Betina, but he asked Lynn to dance. Somehow she found herself out on the dance floor with him and he was inquiring with interest, "Is he in love with you?"

"Who?"

"That...Kevin."

"Of course not," Lynn scoffed.

"He gave me brief but very succinct rules for dancing with you—with a graphic threat if I didn't follow them." Pete watched her face.

"Don't be ridiculous."

Pete looked past her shoulder and reported, "He's moved his chair so he can watch us. I'll turn so you can see, but it'll take a while to get you around, because I have to be careful that my thigh doesn't accidentally brush your skirt." He seemed oddly amused and stimulated at the same time.

"Oh, for heaven's sake!" She was exasperated.

"You want my thigh to brush against you?" He peered into her face in surprise.

"Don't be stupid."

"That's what I'm very earnestly trying not to do. He's big."

All that conversation passed through Lynn's beleaguered brain without really settling anywhere. She was delivered, unbrushed, back to the table, and it was Kevin who seated her close to him.

But she didn't really notice. She was wondering

why Kevin didn't react to Betina. And Betina wasn't flirting with Kevin. That worried her a little. Was there something wrong with Kevin that Betina was ignoring him? How could there be? She studied Kevin and Betina, listened to the table conversation, and gradually it dawned on her that Betina was in love with Marvin! How astonishing. Marvin was very bland and far, far inferior to Kevin. After that she tried to figure out why Betina wouldn't seize the opportunity to abandon Marvin and try for Kevin.

The test was a flop. A complete waste of time. She hadn't learned a thing. Who would ever think Betina, of all people, would settle on one man? The whole evening had been for nothing.

Of course, she had got to dance with Kevin. He was a good dancer. He led well. In control. He moved beautifully. But there was more to life than dancing. Whether he could dance did not have anything to do with his character. It was this she had wanted to expose, not his footwork.

Since the evening was ruined, Lynn determined to get something out of it dancing with Kevin. He didn't appear to mind, either. He held her tightly and plastered her against him, his breathing disturbed, and she was looking a lot like Betina. She relished it.

She knew she bothered him. He was disturbed by her being so close to him. But he could have drawn away and danced more discreetly. He could have done that. He didn't. He pressed her close along his body and his big hand on her back kept her there.

She smiled against his shoulder.

When he finally returned her home, Lynn said good-night inside the street door, but she didn't let him come upstairs. He did suggest it. She couldn't allow that, but she did kiss him.

She kissed that sensual lower lip and indulged her craving for it. She generously included the upper lip, with some added attention to his tongue. Her hands petted the back of his head and she leaned her body into his. She found all that pleasurable. Apparently he did, too.

Kevin held her sweet body to him and ached. She allowed his kisses to deepen, and when she wound her arms around his head he thought his skull would explode with her sweetness, her softness, her eagerness.

But she was very firm that he was not to go upstairs with her. She said a cheerful good-night and closed the door after him, leaving him out in the cold February night.

8

THE DAYS PASSED and Kevin argued for their affair to begin, but she was firmly opposed. It was harder to refuse now because of her gratitude for his care when she had been sick. But, she maintained, one didn't repay favors with one's favors.

He wanted her to go to Anderson and meet his parents, then attend a family reunion and help count his cousins, but she said she couldn't, that she was busy. Meeting his parents was too serious. She was afraid it would seem like some kind of commitment.

He still gave her the kisses of forgetfulness and she knew she really ought to stop these. But she waited for them, longed for them, dreamed of them.

Somehow in that turbulent time they did finish the book. Kevin devised an earthquake that split the cavern. The falling rocks missed everyone but conveniently killed the guard. With superhuman strength, Captain Brick managed to drag the guard's body close enough to get the keys that released their chains. Then Tod rescued Claire.

As the earthquake tremors increased, the two sought shelter in a discreet side tunnel. Lying close together, they made love in the dark, one hundred pages after the first time.

Lynn wasn't sure. "I seriously doubt they'd make love under those violent circumstances."

"Under duress, distraction is essential," Kevin argued.

"Sex would distract them from an earthquake?" She was not convinced.

"Of course."

"That's mad." She was positive about that, anyway.

"Ed loved the idea. You just have to put in how they go about it."

She quoted: "'With the tumbling, unstable mountain threatening to crush their lives away, Tod pulled Claire under him, crushing her....'"

"Great!"

"Ridiculous."

"It can't always be moonlight and roses." He shrugged as one would who accepted circumstances as they were. "Anyway, men are aroused by danger."

"After they've—made love—" she slid it in "—what distracts them if the earthquake isn't finished, too."

He had to smile a little. "Well, at least they have a more relaxed attitude."

She laughed. Then she looked at him and sobered. She put out her hands, palms up. "It's finished."

He started visibly. "What's finished?"

"Your book. When I've written this part, it's done."

"You've woven in all the glances and touches?" he queried.

"You know I have."

"Lynn, I have another book. I've been plotting it out for some time. I've put pages sideways where it seems logical for them to make love."

"Brick?" She winced.

"No. The medical officer."

"A . . . medical officer?" she inquired cautiously.

He went over to the front door and picked up a package from the floor by the coat tree, as he continued offhandedly, "A queasy medical officer." She was silent so he looked up—or at least he raised his head and his eyelashes were aimed her way. "And the woman has short black hair and sherry-brown eyes."

She thought she should protest, or at least demur, but she wasn't sure exactly how to do that.

"They spend all their time on the examination table," he added.

"Researching?" she guessed with a beginning smile.

Straight-faced, he handed her the package and replied, "Diligently."

Lynn undid the rubber bands and took off the bulky cover. She gasped and shot a glance his way, then burst out in helpless laughter. There were as many pages sideways to mark the love scenes as there were of manuscript. She ruffled the marking pages and raised her eyebrows.

"They're attracted," he explained, turning out a hand as if it were obvious.

"Apparently," she commented dryly. "What else is in the manuscript?"

"A lot of glances and touches."

"Anything else?"

"A little dallying," he suggested.

She laughed again. While trying to avoid picturing the actual dalliance between a queasy medic and a dark-haired woman aged thirty-two. "Is this another adventure in the outer reaches of space with an earth-like planet and humanoids?" She began to riffle through the manuscript pages, then stopped abruptly and looked up at Kevin. "They're *all* blank!"

"Yes. Well, you see, I thought if you wrote the love scenes, I'd add the story afterward. Like what we did with the last one but the reverse."

"You want me to write a love story and you'll fill in the chinks with a little sci-fi?" She was not sure she had understood.

"Exactly."

"It's easier to write the story and then add the romance," she objected.

"Is it?" he asked courteously.

"While every story needs romance, not all love stories need sci-fi." It was a statement of fact.

This offended him. "Of course, that's just a matter of opinion ... from a romance writer."

"Any good writer is a romantic. You know that. I write love stories. And judging by the number of blank pages, this is going to be a love story. A long love story."

"I think you've cast a spell on me."

"You're popping out in warts?" she asked brightly. "Flies are beginning to look appetizing?"

"All I can think about is my characters having sex."

Instructing him firmly, she said, "I write about making love. I do not write about sex. Just having sex is a lot different from making love."

"Show me," he urged. "Show me how the Martianlike humanoids on this Marslike planet mate."

She went, "Umph," as if she'd been hit in the stomach.

"I'm a willing student." He gestured, showing his openness. "I think, under the circumstances, it's vital that I know." He deliberately used their running joke to ease the seriousness of his invitation to love. "Teach me."

Against the tide of desire she managed to say, "That would be like teaching a fish to swim, a frog to jump or a bird to . . . ."

"Yeah, go on," he encouraged. "And a bird to what?"

"Cheep?" she offered.

"You were rolling right along there, weren't you, and all of a sudden you had this vision of birds learning to fly. Didn't you?"

She gave him an exasperated look. "The parents teach birds."

"To eat and to keep the nest clean and to fly, but the making love part is always done by an older female bird. It said so in *National Geographic*."

"Nonsense. I never saw anything about that in *National Geographic*."

"You must have missed that issue."

"Baloney." And to quickly change the subject, she said sensibly, "I think what we really need to do is figure out what you're going to write for your next book."

"I haven't settled on the premise." He went over to the window.

She flipped through the ream of blank pages on her lap and said, "Apparently this one's about the vast emptiness of space." She thought this was funny, but he didn't respond.

She tried again. "How about a plague? Or just two people on board—one male and one female— but being in space suits, they don't immediately realize that?"

"How about two writers who collaborate on a book and fall in love?"

The thrill of the thought slid through her, and she had to swallow before she managed to speak. "No one would ever believe that old hack."

He turned and looked at her. "I would."

"That's only because you're unfamiliar with love stories."

"That's true." He moved toward her and she panicked, because she was bogged down in the sofa and there was no quick way to escape. "I'm unfamiliar with love, too," he said in a husky voice.

She tried desperately to distract him. "The plague—it could be something that makes the whole crew think they're in love!"

"Terrific," he intoned as he removed the ream of disassembled papers in her hands and lay them on the floor. Then he sat next to her and took her into his arms.

She stiffened, her hands warding off his, and she said, "And with that—people thinking they're in love—there would be jealousies and fights; and Captain Brick, naturally, would be unaffected, and it would take him a while to understand what was going on. He is a little obtuse."

"He's distracted by the responsibilities of command," Kevin said, while concentrating completely on pulling her closer to him. He did this with great care. Then he kissed her.

The logical part of her mind was drowning in the surging tide of sensation, but she thought; *this is different.* It had not been this way with either Steve or Mark. Why was it different in Kevin's arms? Biological need? It must be her age.

How divinely he held her, how delicious to feel herself respond to him. How wonderful to be kissed by Kevin Walker.

When he lifted his head minutely, his breathing unsteady, she blurted out with a groan, "I love your lower lip. It drives me mad."

Instantly it was against her mouth and he breathed, "It's yours."

She sighed. "Ohhhhh...." And he kissed her again. She said, "Ohhhh," several more times, either aloud or in her throat.

He didn't say anything else. He was very busy. His kisses were so overwhelming that she melted and lay back in a nest of pillows. He had her under him, half-buried in cushions, with her shirt pulled free from her trousers and bunched up around her neck. His mouth was doing all sorts of magical

Harlequin Temptation

Have you ever thought
you were in love
with one man...only
to feel attracted to another?

That's just one of the temptations you'll find facing the women in *Harlequin Temptation* romance novels.

Sensuous ... contemporary ... compelling ... reflecting today love relationships!

The passionate torment of a woma torn between two loves...the sire call of a career...the magnet advances of an impetuous em ployer—nothing is left unexplore in this romantic series fro Harlequin. You'll thrill to a ca did new frankness as men ar women seek to form lastir relationships in the face temptations that threate true love. *Don't miss a sing one!* You can start *Harlequ Temptation* coming to yo home each month for ju $1.75 per book. Beg with your FREE copy First Impressions.

Mail the reply card toda

GET THIS BOOK FREE!

First Impressions
by Maris Soule

He was involved with her best frie Tracy Dexter couldn't deny her attraction her new boss. Mark Prescott looked mc like a jet set playboy than a high sch principal–and he acted like one, too. wasn't right for Tracy to go out with him, when her friend Rose had already stake claim. It wasn't right, even though Mar eyes were so persuasive, his kiss so probi and intense. Even though his han scorched her body with a teasing, rag fire...and when he gently lowered her the floor she couldn't find the words to say n

A word of warning to our regular readers: Wh Harlequin books are always in good taste, yo find more sensuous writing in *Harlequin Temptat* than in other Harlequin romance series.

®™Trademarks of Harlequin Enterprises Ltd.

Exclusive Harlequin home subscriber benefits!
- CONVENIENCE of home delivery
- NO CHARGE for postage and handling
- FREE *Harlequin Romance Digest* ®
- FREE BONUS books
- NEW TITLES 2 months ahead of retail
- A MEMBER of the largest romance fiction book club in the world

GET **FIRST IMPRESSIONS** FREE AS YOUR INTRODUCTION TO *Harlequin Temptation* ™ PLUS A FREE TOTE BAG!

 ® No one touches the heart of a woman quite like Harlequin

YES, please send me FREE and **without obligation** my *Harlequin Temptation* romance novel, *First Impressions* and my FREE tote bag. If you do not hear from me after I have examined my FREE book, please send me 4 new *Harlequin Temptation* novels each month as soon as they come off the press. I understand that I will be billed only $1.75 per book (total $7.00). There are no shipping and handling or any other hidden charges. There is no minimum number of books that I have to purchase. In fact, I may cancel this arrangement at any time. The FREE tote bag and *First Impressions* are mine to keep as a free gift, even if I do not buy any additional books.   142 CIX MDF5

Name _____

Address _____ Apt. No. _____

City _____ State/Prov. _____ Zip/Postal Code _____

Signature (If under 18, parent or guardian must sign.)

This offer is limited to one order per household and not valid to present *Harlequin Temptation* subscribers. We reserve the right to exercise discretion in granting membership.

PRINTED IN U.S.A.

Get this romance novel and tote bag
FREE as your introduction to

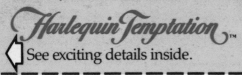

Harlequin Temptation ™

◁ See exciting details inside.

things to her throat and ear and nipples when they both became aware of the doorbell's insistent buzz. They separated just enough to look at each other, unbelieving.

She gasped in a whisper, "This sort of thing happens only in books to save the heroine's virtue."

"Ignore the bell." He moved his face into the curve of her throat.

But she straight-elbowed him, then turned her head when that didn't work and said urgently, "It might be my mother or one of my sisters... and they have keys!" It was as though she had been hit with a bucket of cold water.

"You gave them keys? What a stupid thing to do!" he exclaimed crossly as he rose and ran his hands roughly through his hair.

She struggled to rise as the buzzer sounded again, and he automatically put out a hand to help her up. She hurried to the window that he had unstuck, opened it and yelled down, "Who is it?" as she frantically straightened her shirt.

From below a deep voice floated up, "It's Rick. May I have five pieces of wood from your wood-pile?"

"Take the whole pile if you need it," Lynn called back.

"I think five pieces will last long enough. I've convinced Marge to come for dinner to talk things over."

"Good luck!"

He called his thanks, and Lynn closed the window. Feeling awkward, she turned back to confront

Kevin, who was still right where she had left him. He looked as if he had barely survived a strong wind. A shyness crept into her manner and she heard herself say, "You look as if you've been assaulted."

Without spaces between the words, he replied, "Not-enough-who's-Rick?"

Feeling uncertain, still shocked that her reaction to Kevin had got so out of hand and embarrassed by this, Lynn seized on the distraction. "You're a writer. What do you think?"

He thought for a minute as he watched her, and he understood she needed to take an emotional step back from him. He helped her do this by going along with her conversational ploy. "He and his wife had a quarrel and she moved out. He's lured her into an intimate dinner back at their place."

What other man, interrupted in the middle of a passionate embrace, would allow the woman to back off with such grace, Lynn wondered, and her voice was gentle as she said, "That isn't it. Try again."

"They're not married and she wanted a permanent relationship. That is, she's moved out until he will consent to marry her?"

"That's the same basic theme." She could smile in his direction, but her eyes sought other places in the room.

He was so intently aware of every nuance in her expression that his mind was only partly on the conversation. "He asked for the wood, and you offered him the whole pile. Is he out of a job?"

"That's better," she encouraged. "And Marge?"

"Not his wife?"

She shook her head.

"Why a cozy dinner at his place if it's business?" Kevin pondered that. "He's in the arts."

"Good." She was so very aware of him. She began to tidy things about the room so that she could turn and give him longer glances. Her movements were self-conscious and just a bit jerky.

"An actor?" He looked at her walls. "An artist."

She took up the explanation, using the telling as an excuse to study him very seriously. "Marge is thinking of sponsoring him. She's going to look at a million paintings tonight." She caught the outrageous exaggeration. "Or maybe almost a hundred and her mind will reel." As Lynn's own mind did, looking at Kevin. "And she'll be so impressed that she will have to see his work again and she'll be convinced. He did one of her. A painting of her," Lynn tacked on.

"That was very bright." Kevin sounded a little distracted.

"She'll never recognize herself in the painting until he tells her. She'll be so intrigued when he gives it to her that she'll take it home and stare at it for a long time, trying to figure it out, and she'll be trapped."

He nodded, not really interested. "She'll be his patron."

"Well, I don't think she'll contribute financially, but she will introduce him to people who can arrange shows for him," Lynn said earnestly. "And becoming known is essential for the artist. I have

one of his pictures. It's one of the climbing people.''
She moved to the stair door and opened it, and as he
came toward her her lips parted and her bosom
swelled.

Her tongue took over and she rushed into speech.
''When I move out of here, do you realize what it's
going to cost me to replace that wall so I can take the
climbing people with me? I'll probably live in a one-
story house and I'll have to build a bell tower to re-
construct the mural so that all the artists can come
back and see it again and remember that utterly mad
night.''

''Which one?'' Kevin stood close to her, looking
down at her.

She swallowed. ''The night of the Fine Arts Ball,
when everyone came here afterward and they all
painted—''

''Which figure?'' he asked. His hands slid into his
pockets as he dragged his eyes from her in order to
look down the stairwell.

''The most bizarre one. I believe it was a self-
portrait.''

First she had him look at all the figures again in
order to judge for himself which one was Rick's.
There was a choice, but he narrowed it down to two.
Then he did choose the correct one.

Kevin looked up and down the stairs and asked
Lynn, ''Did you . . . model for any of these?''

''Little Lynn model?'' She spread one hand on her
chest. ''Surely you jest?'' She could flirt with him
again, but cautiously.

''Modest?''

"No one asked," she admitted.

"You would have?" He snapped his eyelashes her way.

"No. But it would have been nice to be asked. I had my refusal all ready and never could use it." Feeling easier with him, she stuck out her own lower lip in a pout.

"Your lower lip drives me mad." He gathered her to him and kissed her very sweetly.

She kissed him back, but that was a very dangerous thing to do on stairs. When Kevin kissed her her equilibrium wasn't reliable on a solid floor, much less on the stairs.

After a while she managed to say softly, "You should go home. The weather report says we could get some ice." She was standing on the stair above him, so she was an inch or so taller, and she touched the rims of his ears with slow relishing fingers.

"We still have to talk about the new book," he reminded her.

"You gave me a stack of blank pages."

"That was just to get your attention and to show you that I'm becoming a love-story devotee."

"On two books?" she managed to scoff.

"I went to the bookstore and ordered all your books and I read them," he told her.

"And..." she prompted.

"And you drive me right up the wall," he growled.

"Just with the books? You must be especially susceptible," she said. "Reading for aliens to this planet, must be like measles were for the Indians. And you have no natural immunity."

"Yes." He kissed along her jaw and his voice rumbled. "I would like to live with you and be your love, and you could benefit from this in boundless ways."

"I could?" She leaned back comfortably in his hard arms and made his hair into horns on the side of his head.

"There'd be more material for love scenes for your books."

"How kind of you to want to help," she commended, again teasing him in a very comfortable way.

"It's second nature for those in the brotherhood of writers to help one another."

"'Brotherhood'?" she repeated, questioning the use of that particular word.

"Companionhood? Loverhood?" he amended.

"I think you ought to leave now. You're getting mushy."

"You did notice?" He acted impressed.

She didn't reply but moved back up the stairs. When he followed, she stopped and commanded, "No. Go...home!"

"Without my coat?"

"Stay right there, and I'll hand your coat to you."

"I have the distinct impression you don't really trust me," he ventured thoughtfully.

"How astute." She went through the door and grabbed his coat from the rack and pushed it at him. "Goodbye." But she smiled.

"No wonder no one asked you to model. You probably have rivets in your seams."

"You guessed!"

"Kiss me goodbye very sweetly," he commanded, "or I'll throw myself down the stairs, break my leg and have to live with you for six weeks like *The Man Who Came to Dinner.*"

"That's blackmail." She stepped down closer to him.

He smiled benignly and he leaned forward to make his mouth convenient.

"If I kiss you—" and she knew she wanted it "—you will remember that I am doing this under duress?"

"Absolutely."

"And you will realize that I'm not encouraging you in any way?"

"But if it's going to be a decent kiss, you have to make it seem as if you like it."

"I'm not sure I can do that," she leveled with him. "I've never been very good at acting."

"Try," he encouraged. "You'll have to do it until you get it right."

She managed to heave a large sigh of resignation as she said, "Anything for peace and quiet." And she tried to appear reluctant, when she could hardly wait to get her hands on him.

She looked at him and could detect a gleam behind those lashes as he waited for her. She leaned closer, her eyes drawn to that enticing lower lip, and anticipation surged up in her body in thrilling spirals that touched sensitive places and set off quiverings of desire.

She hesitated. She really ought not to kiss him. She ought to draw back or just kiss his cheek, but

what she really ought to do would be to step back
inside her apartment, slam the door and lock it!

That's what she ought to do all right. But her
lips parted and her body urged her closer to him,
and their disturbed breaths mingled as their lips
touched.

Their arms closed around each other, and their
bodies molded themselves against each other as their
kiss fused hotly. They were right back to where they
had been before Rick interrupted, and it was a
wonder they didn't tumble down the stairs. She
gasped against his mouth and groaned, and he just
breathed harshly as they continued the greedy kiss.

Finally they parted out of sheer exhaustion and
leaned against the walls, trying to orient themselves.
"I believe you have a future in the theater," Kevin
said.

Trying to act casual, Lynn lifted a hand to her
hair, but the hand trembled and forgot the original
instructions, going to her swollen, eager mouth, instead. Her fingers comforted it for being without his.

"Shall I come by tomorrow?" He had to clear his
throat.

"Um."

His voice roughened and he told her, "You are so
beautiful." His hunger for her made her appear especially vivid. Her eyes were deep and clear, the lids
heavy, and her mouth was so tempting. "I have to
give you the kiss of forgetfulness..." he began, and
his voice was not steady.

She met him halfway. It really was a kiss of forgetfulness, because she forgot where she was; forgot

all her firm resolutions, all her past disastrous deal-
ings with two very charming, equally enticing men.
And she forgot to be careful.

She wound herself around him and encouraged
him to think whatever he liked. She cooperated and
entered the embrace with unbridled enthusiasm. But
when she was in a total shambles and would have
turned and led him back into the apartment, Kevin
broke the kiss and set her away from him. She
looked at him blankly.

"I've got to leave," he panted.

Baffled, she tried to sort out such remarkable behavior, but it was beyond her.

He patted her shoulder and said, "I just hope I can
walk." Then he turned and stumbled down the
stairs and out of sight.

She was sure he would come back. She stood
there, waiting, but he didn't return. Her arms moved
as if on uncertain strings, bringing her fingers up
first to console her stomach, then to touch her swollen breasts. When they reached her bereft mouth
they lingered there. He was gone.

Eventually she went into her apartment, put on
her jogging suit and left by way of the windswept
back stairs. She ran in a loose, flopping way and forgot the exercise stops.

9

IT WAS THE PERSISTENT CLICKING of ice against the windows that finally caught Lynn's attention. She went over and looked out, amazed by how quickly the ice was covering the ground. March was coming in like a lion.

How long had it been sleeting? She had no idea. She tried to recall how the weather had been when she was jogging, but she couldn't. Her thoughts had been only of Kevin.

It was a good thing he'd been smart enough to leave. If she'd had her way, she would have dragged him back inside the apartment and right now they'd be in that bed, asleep from exhaustion. Her mouth joined her body in a wrenching, muted wail of regret.

She really wanted him. Never had she had to cope with such a hunger. Kevin had aroused her to a fever pitch and she wanted him.

She could have him. She could handle an affair. Why not? She was certainly no nubile neophyte. She was an adult, responsible for herself. She understood all the risks and ramifications of an affair, and she could keep her emotions separate and free of entanglement. She could do that.

She wasn't dumb. She had learned her lessons well. She could enjoy him physically, keeping things light and cheerful. She would make it very clear to him that it was all just a lark. She could do that.

And she would protect him from any emotional entrapment, too. She would be considerate because she knew how awful the consequences could be.

Going to her closet, she looked over her wardrobe—sweaters, slacks and a flannel robe. She needed to buy something sexy. Slinky lounging pajamas, maybe. And some lacy things to entice him, though he didn't seem to need a whole lot of enticing. He appeared to have a natural inclination.

As the ice continued to rap on the windows, she eyed her wood, piled in the holder by the fireplace, and figured she had enough for three days if she was frugal. Three days? What if he couldn't get back the next day the way he said he would? She'd have to get through not one but three whole ghastly long days? Damn.

And she had insisted he leave! Mad. She was absolutely, idiotically mad. He would have been willing, and if she hadn't been so incredibly stupid, he would still be there and they would be in that cozy bed in each other's arms, their naked bodies close and rubbing minutely together....

She paced the room in agitation, but eventually she convinced herself that it was all for the best. God knew what being susceptible to men had done to her life and to her emotional well-being. She was right to be cautious. It was just as well Rick had interrupted them and she'd sent Kevin off so she had the time to think out this whole relationship.

She did want him. She wanted no part of any commitment, and she would make that clear, but why struggle against mutual attraction that was just physical? They weren't school kids. She was thirty-two and self-supporting, and he was almost thirty. That was old enough for a mature relationship.

The remembrance intruded of his having to lie down when she'd cut her hand. She smiled faintly and ran a finger over the scar. And she recalled how sweet he had been when she was sick. He was a gentle man. He was a superior man. If she were susceptible to marriage, she would consider him. Snare him. But she was not, and she would not.

Then her mind focused on his eyelashes. What daughters he would have! They would drive men wild with eyelashes like Kevin's. And his sensual lower lip. His sons would be equally devastating. It would be interesting to see his children. She would... she would what? She would be interested, as an observer, that was all. An observer.

She went back to the front window and looked pensively down on the street, which was rapidly being covered with a thick layer of ice pellets. There was no traffic. She went to the radio and turned on the weather station, where a calm voice warned people to stay home. She switched it off and knew herself to be trapped alone in that apartment for at least a couple of days. Restlessly she returned to the windows and watched an ice-covered car inching along as some nut tried to move on the impossible street. People could be so stupid.

She watched through the thick veil of sleet as the car struggled against the ice; the windshield was coated in spite of the efforts of the wipers. The car slithered to the curb and became immobile. She wondered what the person would do?

She saw the car door open and a figure emerge. How could he get help? No one could get through that storm to help. The man locked the car door and turned toward her apartment house. Then she lost sight of whoever it was.

Everything was turning white and the wind was calm. She looked out on the arcticscape and was thinking how it must have been for the pioneers when her doorbell sounded. The nut had come to her door? Of all the doors around why...and then she went still and strained to scrutinize the ice-covered car. Not allowing herself to hope, she ran down the stairwell and flung open the door.

It was Kevin.

Grabbing his arm, she pulled him into the entryway and eyed him hungrily. He grinned, closed the door and turned her to go up the stairs. He said to her, "I had a hell of a time getting back here."

"'Getting back'?" She paused.

He took her arm and urged her on. "I knew this storm was coming, so I went to that ice-cream place over on Rudisil to wait until it got bad enough to be stranded, but it came down faster than I thought it would."

"You plotted being stranded here?" She peeked up at him.

"Oh, yes," he admitted readily.

"How wicked of you!"

"Yes." He said, well pleased with himself.

They reached the top of the stairs and entered the apartment. She closed the door and leaned against it.

She had him! He was there, and he could not leave, and she had him.

He didn't look terribly alarmed. In fact, he smiled down at her as he removed his coat. He hung it on the rack and turned to her. She looked into his eyes and smiled back at him, running her hands under his sweater to lift it. She watched his expression change as he realized she was going to peel it off him. He helped.

Then she went to work on his shirt. He allowed her to do that alone, watching her face and waiting for the times she glanced up at him. She felt the color darken her throat and creep up her cheeks and pretended that it was from the struggle she was having undressing him.

She knew it was better to wait and not be in such a rush, that she should pause and savor and anticipate. She understood that was the way to do it, but her greedy fingers just hurried along and she was caught up in their excitement.

She was panting a little, breathing through parted lips as she knelt down to remove his shoes. He put a hand against the wall for balance as she lifted his foot and began to peel off his sock.

Amused, he said, "I had no idea you were in such a state. I believe it's a good thing I came back. Think of you ranging around this apartment, locked in here by an ice storm and not even being able to get out to jog."

"I did jog," she told him breathlessly.

"It never really helps," he sympathized. "It's like cold showers."

"I've found that out."

"Want me, do you." He was unforgivably smug.

"A little," she admitted.

"A little! My God, I'm hardly inside the door! Are you going to ravish me right here? Or will we make it to the bed?"

"I'm not sure," she stated earnestly as she worked feverishly on the other sock.

"I believe I've probably frozen to death and this is a dying hallucination," he speculated.

She threw the sock aside and reached up to undo his belt. His face became serious. She unzipped his pants and slid them off his hips. She had a little trouble getting them down, but she finally managed and slid them off his legs. He stepped free of them, to stand naked before her. She sat there on her heels, her hands on her knees, and looked up at him. He watched her looking.

He was just so beautifully masculine. How awful to put clothes on that magnificent male form.

She leaned forward and ran her hands up his hair-textured thighs to his body and he couldn't hold still any longer. He reached his hands down under her armpits and dragged her up the length of his body. His kiss melded them—their tongues touching, their breaths furnace blasts, their bodies trembling with desire.

His hands shook as he fumbled with her clothes. She hurried herself out of them, not distracted by

Collaboration

the removal, as she fought to be naked against him,
to touch and kiss him, aware only that he was there
and her body was going wild with wanting him.

Her hands were everywhere on him, clutching
and pressing and feeling him as his own squeezed
and rubbed. His strong arms held her to him as they
appeared to struggle to fuse their bodies and become
one entity.

He lifted her and she wrapped her legs around
him, locking her heels in back of him, as their
mouths fed on each other. He carried her to the bed
and lay her there, then eased down on top of her.
Their need was so urgent he entered her at once. Her
arms and legs wrapped around him and she groaned
with the force of the passion that assailed her as she
engulfed his body, clinging to his rhythm. They
went wild in their ride. Their moans and sighs mingled and the sounds of their ecstasy were gasped
with ragged breaths as they flew off the edge and,
clinging only to each other, reached a thrilling peak.
And they found paradise before they floated slowly
back to reality.

They didn't talk for a while but lay there smiling
at each other. She made throaty sounds and petted
him with tiny strokes, smoothing his hair, sliding
her hand along his cheek and running it in slow caressing circles on his shoulder.

He didn't mind. He was sleepy and contented, and
he looked like a lion that had eaten too much wilde-
beest. He teased her in a languid voice. "We made it
to the bed! What slowed you down? I was sure I'd be
had right there in the doorway."

She made a soft response that sounded like a cross between a hum and a chuckle.

"You female humanoids are wild! How do the males survive?"

"We come into heat only once a year," she explained lazily. "You just happened to catch me at the right time."

"You mean I have to wait for a year?" He almost raised himself up, but it was just a token move.

"Um-hm."

"Well...I think it'll be worth it." He yawned and smiled at her.

"You are fabulous," she murmured.

"How could you tell? It all happened so fast I'm not sure if it did. As soon as I can hold my eyes open we'll have to have a slow-motion replay so I can see what happened."

"How can you tell if your eyes are open?" she wanted to know. "They look like solid eyelashes to me."

"When they're open, silly girl, I can see."

"Open them," she commanded.

He did widely, and there were those jewels of warm smoke.

"Does it startle you to see the bare world?" she inquired.

"I am thrilled to see a bare Lynn." His eyes disappeared behind the lash thicket again as he smiled. He put his hand on the side of her head with infinite tenderness. Then she watched him as he fell into a sound sleep. Out cold. She covered him with the down comforter and tucked it gently around his bare shoulders. She studied him, relishing the freedom to do this. Then she got up and went to shower.

Lynn flicked through her closet again wishing she had something slinky and lacy to wear but settling for a red sweater and white slacks. She took pains with makeup and brushed her hair vigorously before she used the curling iron to aid her "ducktails."

She set wood in the fireplace, ready to light, then went in to see what sort of feast she could make to revive her valiant warrior. *Wait a minute,* she told herself, *don't get silly about this little episode.* "Episode"? Event! She leaned against the counter in the kitchen and smiled out at the sleet. *Lovely ice.*

Among the few things in the freezer was a single steak. She would give it to him, and she would have peanut butter. Her mental monitor pointed out the inequity of the diets she was setting up but she reasoned that Kevin had to keep his strength up. They would be stuck here—together—for several days.

Then she felt a strong sense of foreboding about her set course. But she derided it, arguing, why not take advantage of him? He would be there just going to waste, so to speak. And she would simply have a good time getting a lot of frustration out of her system harmlessly.

"Harmlessly"? Was she sure? Sure. No problem. She could handle it. Was she positive? Absolutely!

When the nagging questions lingered, Lynn was harsh in silencing them. She knew what she was doing. But her mind kept printing out question marks as if it were the screen of a computer.

So she went to her processor and typed out: "I am

in control." And the words sat there on the screen. She indicated to her brain that it should take note. She was in control of herself. But creeping like smoke through a crack came the image of frantically disrobing Kevin at the door.

When she typed a second "I am in control," her brain asked who she was trying to convince.

She cleared the screen and sat there stiffly, telling herself she did not need the words printed out in order to believe them. She knew exactly what she was doing. She was indulging her starved senses. Sex was natural. Kevin was a superb, delicious and willing partner.

She was acutely aware he had said nothing of love or of anything that sounded even close to an involvement, and that was exactly the way she wanted it. They could have this interlude, enjoy it and part. It was no big deal. She was going to do it her way.

She went in, stood by *her* bed and looked down at Kevin, who was sleeping peacefully. He was beautiful. It was a totally unemotional observation—simply aesthetic admiration.

She spent some time in her art appreciation, then found herself musing about what God had been up to when He gave Kevin those eyelashes and that lower lip. And that humor and imagination? And that body? It seemed like an awful lot of pluses for one man.

She sat down on the edge of her bed and reached out a hand to lightly brush his hair away from his forehead. His eyelashes quivered, so she knew she had wakened him. He reached a lazy hand up, capturing hers and carrying it to his mouth to press it against his lips. "You're dressed."

"You've been asleep for ages," she told him softly.

"How long?"

"Oh, forty-five minutes, anyway." She smiled at him, there in her bed.

"You knocked me out. It was a little like being hit by a small but fancy car." He smiled back at her. "Or a Mack truck."

"It's not terribly erotic to compare a woman to a Mack truck," she objected. "And it makes you seem like such a victim. But you didn't struggle at all!"

"Who had time?" he protested. "I was literally taken by complete surprise."

"You plotted to come back."

"Yes," he admitted. "But I had all this coaxing and cajoling and seduction in mind, and I never stood a chance! You snatched me inside and stripped me bare and you ravished me!"

"That's what comes of fooling around with older women."

"I should have heard about it sooner." He turned over on his back and stretched, keeping hold of her hand so she was drawn down onto the bed. "All boys should know about older women. I'm surprised no one ever told me."

"Shouldn't you call your parents?" she suggested.

"To tell them I've been ravished by an older woman?" He appeared surprised.

"No, idiot," she scolded softly. "So they won't worry."

"It's too late now." He grinned. "And they don't

know about you, anyway, so why would they worry? I did survive."

She gestured impatiently. "When you don't get back home...with this storm."

"I'm not due there," he explained. "They aren't expecting to see me."

She eyed him. "I thought you lived with them."

"Well, not exactly."

"Aha!" she exclaimed. "When did you land, Martian?"

He had to yawn before he could reply. "Oh, it's been a while. We have to be set up long enough to have Earth people accept us as being normal and to treat us as natives."

"You Martians must make love sometime. How?"

"The women are totally unreceptive and simply submit."

"Aw," she crooned in mock sympathy.

"You're a revelation," he told her. "You say it hits once a year?"

"Um."

"How in the world am I going to survive for twelve endless months or three hundred sixty-four more days?" He leaned over her and nuzzled her face and throat, moving his face slowly over her in sensuous enjoyment. She allowed that.

"You're like silk." His voice was husky. "Since you're just lying there, doing nothing with it, do you mind if I use your body?"

"For what?"

"To...uh...compare it—clinically, of course—to the Martian body. A scientific investigation."

"How intimate have you been with Martian women?" She was curious to see how he would reply.

"I've seen pictures," he confessed candidly. He pulled her sweater up and was distracted by her bare breasts, on which he then lavished his attention.

"Oh," she gasped. Then she breathed, "Ooo-oooo."

"Do you like that?" he asked with intense interest.

"Um."

"Martian women have great big ones, but they won't let you touch them. Or so I've heard," he added hastly.

"Why not?"

"I never found out," he replied readily. "Let's see what's down here." He undid her slacks and eased them off. "What do you know!" he exclaimed. "White cotton underwear!" He aimed his eyelashes her way.

"They're practical," she defended. *Like the Speedo practice suit,* she groaned inwardly.

"Practical...and sexy."

"'Sexy'?" Her voice was unbelieving, and she blushed, embarrassed.

"Is there any other kind of underwear?" he asked innocently. "Wool would itch." He removed the white cotton and lay his hand on her bare stomach. "You'd hate to itch there, wouldn't you?" He smiled.

She tried not to grin. Her heart had picked up its beat and her breathing was quicker. He leaned over and kissed her stomach, which got excited. Then he licked her navel with slow lion laps. That sent sky-rockets shooting off throughout her body and rack-eting around, so that her stomach fluttered and her bones wobbled and her breasts rose.

But this was absurd. She was replete. There was no way she could become aroused again. She took hold of his head and lifted it so she could look into his eyes and said, "Quit teasing. I'm sated. There's no way I could do it again."

"That's okay. I'm just making this scientific inves-tigation...." He kissed the wrists of her restraining hands and then went back to work on her navel. Be-tween laps, he said, "Just lie back and don't worry. Thorough investigations take time. You wouldn't want me to do a slipshod job of it, would you? I might miss something." And he gave her stomach another lick for good measure.

He was very thorough. He explored and investi-gated and commented. He kissed and savored every inch of her until she gasped and squirmed and groaned with exquisite delight.

"There is one final part of the investigation and then we'll rest," he said. "For a while." His voice was soft and deep.

"What more?" she whispered, her heart pound-ing.

So he showed her. He slid onto her and joined with her. Then he moved in slow delicious ways. He built a need in her that took over her brain, render-ing it useless, and she tried to hurry him, but he would not be hurried.

"I thought you did this only once a year," he chided. "Here you've lulled me into a false sense of security, thinking I was safe, and look at you!"

Then she recognized that she had become pretty frantic, so she made herself stop and hold still. But he moved again—insidiously—and set her off once more. He laughed in his throat, kissed her and rolled over, holding her to him so that they couldn't be separated. And he teased her. She loved it.

She slowed down, and their lovemaking reached another plateau of sensual delight, different from anything she had known possible. Each move was exquisite. Each touch was savored; each kiss was a shared thrill as their arousal was at fever pitch and they rode a fine line of mind-bending pleasure. He held them there very carefully, allowing them neither to falter nor to soar too high. It was as if nothing else existed in all the world.

He was a master, and he guided her to relish each nuance of their enchantment. Worshipping her body, he showed her the rapture of his. And he led her along uncharted paths of bliss before they shared the heights.

At last, they lay spent and unmoving, holding hands. They were dazed from the scope of their experience. After a long time Lynn murmured, "I had no idea it could be this way."

"Me, neither." He lifted his free hand as if by remote control, and it traveled over the short distance and settled on the top of her hand sandwiching it, between his.

In a while she said, "It's pretty...awesome."

He replied an understanding, "Um."

"I feel a little like crying, and I'm not sure why."

With great lethargy, Kevin moved to take her into his arms. He settled her close until she was snuggly cuddled against him, then said, "Cry if you like. Just don't attack me again for a little while."

"I didn't attack you that time," she reminded him. "It was your scientific investigation that got out of hand."

"Is that what happened?" He didn't actually appear very curious. "I feel as if I've been had."

"I suspect you've done this before."

"I may have had sex—" he had turned serious "—but I've never made love this way. What a fantastic experience. You're incredible."

"I only went along for the ride...."

"What a beautiful ride." He kissed her forehead chastely.

"What a stingy kiss! Why aren't you kissing me erotically? That isn't the way you were kissing me just a little while ago. What happened to your ardor?"

"I don't know. It's mysteriously dissipated." He moved a hand up to gesture, and it dropped tiredly back to her shoulder. "I believe I shall close my eyes for a minute or two." He tucked the comforter around them carefully, gave her forehead another brotherly kiss, and they both went to sleep.

When they awoke wind was buffeting the house and causing it to shudder. They looked at each other with some awkwardness, acutely conscious of their new intimacy. He grinned at her and said, "I've been

here for almost five hours. Could I please get out of
bed for a while?"

She sat up slowly and smiled at him with an odd
shyness as she winced a bit over the tenderness of
her well-loved body. He appeared completely recovered, but she was stiff. He moved her from the
bed and into the bathroom, where he bathed her
sweetly. He dried her, amused by her languid responses. Retrieving her clothes from where he had
discarded them, he dressed her. His things were in
the living room by the front door.

Clothed, they stood looking out the living-room
windows onto the wind-driven world. The storm had
closed down the winter day, but the ice-covered
world reflected light and it was strangely bright out. It
continued to sleet. The fine pellets tapped on the windows, building up on the ledges and on the ground.

Lynn had put the steak in a plastic bag in cold
water and it was thawed. He inspected it dubiously.
"Will you share with me?"

"It's yours," she replied.

"Oh? I thought it was your dinner. I can't eat
your steak."

"It's yours," she repeated. "You may be here for a
day or two and you have to... keep up your strength."
She looked up at him innocently and bit her lower lip
to keep from smirking.

He laughed aloud and ruffled her hair. "Thaw me
another."

"That's the only one."

"I'm not going to eat the whole thing," he insisted. "You have it."

"We'll share," she decided. "I'm not hungry and I know you must be starved."

"Ravenous," he admitted.

"Start with half a grapefruit."

They opened the drop-leaf table in the living room and placed it by the fire. They concocted a smorgasbord that was diverse and imaginative, and as they snacked they chatted and laughed managing to eat quite a lot.

They discussed being snowbound and invented all sorts of plots that could arise from two people being held isolated by the weather. The time passed quickly, and they were astounded when they realized how late it was.

In bed they snuggled in each others' arms, and it was lovely. Lynn sighed and wiggled, and Kevin said, "Forget it." She giggled and wiggled, and he told her to be still and be quiet. Finally she settled down, and they slept.

10

THE NEXT MORNING they wakened early, to study each other with smiles and touches. Then they got up to shower and dress. Lynn pulled on a deep-gold sweater and light-gray slacks. Kevin made a show of debating over what to wear, then wore the only clothes he had with him.

Sitting crowded together at the little kitchen table, he asked her over their eggs, "Would you ever have given in if I hadn't come back yesterday?"

"After you left," she confided, "I decided, 'Why not?' I wanted you and you did seem willing."

"You noticed that?"

"Not from anything you did or said, but I suspected you just might...cooperate."

He grinned. "And have you found me satisfactorily cooperative?"

"No," she stated. "You just lie there and make me do all the work."

He laughed. Then he reached over and kissed her cheek. "So you decided you wanted me?" He was like a big purring cat who was being scratched behind his ear.

"In this neighborhood of old people and college

students there isn't just a whole lot of available material..." she began with studied indifference.

"You're a spider waiting for an unwary wasp?" he asked.

"I noticed the stinger."

"Good grief! Do you mean to tell me that women ogle men?" He spread his hand on his chest in an elaborate parody of shock.

"Who could miss those eyelashes?" she teased, deliberately misunderstanding.

"I trimmed them once when I was about...oh, I must have been nine or ten. All the old ladies—who were in their thirties or so—" he slid a look at her "—kept carrying on about my eyelashes. So I got the scissors and cut them down. My mother did a double take when she saw me. She said, 'What's the matter, son, are you all right? Has something scared you?' Then she looked at me again and she screamed, 'What happened to your eyelashes?'

"I thought they were a pain at the time. But after that girls my age and older women of fourteen and fifteen would smile and tell me, 'Oh, those eyelashes,' so I thought maybe they weren't quite such a curse after all."

Curious, she had to ask, "When you cut them, could you see better?"

"Without my eyelashes," he replied solemnly "the world is a blatant place—stark and bare."

"Do I look fuzzy to you? Like I'm standing behind bushes?"

"No," he complained. "You're covered with clothes,

though. Why in the world would you hide that gorgeous body behind clothes? How selfish of you."

"You want me to parade around naked in this weather?" She had trouble believing that. "It's winter!"

"Not outside, just here in the apartment—for me."

"I can barely move because of you," she groaned.

"That's just stiff muscles. You have to act exactly as if you'd been thrown from a horse—" he began.

"I feel as if I've been thrown by a horse."

"And get right back on," he finished.

"Forget it."

"It'll loosen you up and oil all your joints and make you loose and pliable again," he assured her. "I had no idea you could be triggered so easily. I've been so careful of you, trying to build up to it slowly, just to get you to think about me. I spent so much energy plotting strategies, and here you are, a sex maniac! Look at the time I've wasted!"

"It's your lower lip," she confided.

"I thought it was my eyelashes." He looked a little indignant.

"The lower lip."

"How have you managed to keep your hands off me up until yesterday?"

"I was very busy keeping your hands off me," she reminded him.

"But that's half the battle—enticing me. And I was enticed," he assured her needlessly. "I thought that if I got back here I'd work for a couple of days, sneaking kisses and maybe a squeeze here and there, and slowly convince you. I sat there in that ice-cream parlor trying to judge the sleet and deciding what approach I'd use—"

"It just astounds me that you could plot a seduction in an ice-cream parlor!" she interrupted. "It's like thinking about sex while you're watching a Disney cartoon! It's really a little kinky."

"I know. A bar would have had a better atmosphere and a whiskey would have given me more courage than two scoops of almond praline, but the bars weren't open yet. Anyway, a sign of maturity is being able to adjust to one's surroundings."

"So you deliberately set out to get stranded here." She shook her head and clucked at him.

"Are you kidding? When the chance of a lifetime came in the form of an ice storm? Do you think an opportunity like that knocks twice? One scrambles to take advantage of the situation."

She just smiled, amused by him.

As if imparting a vital piece of information he informed her, "It wasn't a new diet you needed to improve your disposition and put roses in your cheeks. It was plain, old, ordinary, everyday sex. And fortunately for you you don't have to go out in this storm and search for any. You have a supply readily at hand."

She lay a bold hand on him and he drew in a deep, startled, pleased breath. His hand quickly covered hers, pressing it against him as he closed the short space between them and kissed her gently. It was a lovely squishy kiss, and she flicked her tongue along that lower lip in a sweet caress. He purred deep in his chest and his arms snaked around her, pulling her against him so she was crushed in a boa-constrictor embrace. The air went out of her lungs and her breasts swelled against him, taut and pushy. She laughed throatily as her silly, sated body pretended to want him again.

Briefly delaying his consumption of her, he raised his head to ask, "What's so funny?"

"It's ridiculous, but you're making my insides shiver." She laughed soundlessly and took his sweet breath in gulps, thinking that her dizziness must be caused by breathing secondhand air.

"Shivering?" he rumbled. "That's serious."

"No, it just proves my body doesn't respond logically."

Very slowly he moved his lips and breath over her mouth, then along her face and down her ear. "Your body is brilliant. It wants me. I'm glad I made it back here."

"This is a golden opportunity—" she mumbled.

"Perfect," he agreed.

"To get to work on your new book," she finished.

Kevin pulled back to fix her with an incredulous stare. "Work? On the book? I'm going to spend the entire time working on you! What a strange woman you are!"

"That sentence is supposed to read, 'Strange, what a woman you are,'" she corrected him.

He smiled. "There's the romance novel and then there's the novel romance."

"Right." She had her head on his shoulder, gazing contentedly out the window at the snow, which was now falling softly in a wind-driven swirl. "It's snowing."

Reluctantly he turned his eyes to the window and agreed. Then he exclaimed, "Snow on top of the ice! I'll be here for the rest of the month!" He moved pleasured hands over her and kissed her forehead.

She groaned elaborately.

"Let's stack the dishes in the sink," he suggested, rising.

"Never! What sort of slob would do a thing like that?" She got up, too, and began to clear the table.

"Let's soak them for an hour or so." He slid his hand along her back.

"No, no. We'll wash them immediately." She pushed up her sleeves.

"I didn't mean for you to swing the other way entirely and become a dishwashing fanatic!" he protested.

She retorted primly, "One cannot be wishy-washy about dishes."

He stared.

"I'll wash. You dry." She was bustling around efficiently.

"One must be wary of one's influence," he said in awe.

"You 'only pointed out the areas for improvement,'" she quoted him.

He looked disgusted as he surveyed the kitchen. "This shouldn't take more than ten minutes."

"I have to clean the oven," she announced.

"Today?" He was flabbergasted.

She gave him a placid look. "And then I have to scrub the floor."

His lashes narrowed. "You're trying to weasel out of going back to bed. You're inventing chores!"

"You told me—"

"I have a big mouth," he interrupted crossly. "The crust in the oven has to be sterile."

"What about the floor?"

He looked down at the floor and then took a few tentative steps. "I can unstick my feet without struggling un—"

"You beast!" she proclaimed stridently. "I scrubbed it on my knees yesterday!" She marched over to the stove and opened the oven. "Look!"

He bent down and inspected it. "It's clean."

"It has been all along! My mother was a nut about dirty ovens!"

"And your first husband," he put in.

"I've had only one husband. Mark dropped me before we were married."

"I'd like to meet him," Kevin stated seriously.

She shot him a quick glance. "They're coming back to Fort Wayne. You may well meet."

"I would like to come face to face with any man who'd been that close to possessing you and was fool enough to give you up. It's beyond my comprehension. Does he appear to be normal?"

In the midst of her thrilled reaction to his words she asked cautiously, "Possession?"

"Having exclusive rights?"

"I am not chattel." She took a step away from him.

"I'd put a collar on you and a very short chain."

"Oh, no, you would not!"

"Handcuffs?" He was willing to bargain.

She shook her head and pulled her mouth into a tight line.

"How about a silken rope?" He was being accommodating.

"Nothing." She washed a dish and put it in the drainer.

"You don't want to wear anything? Well, you darling girl, we can fix that right away."

"Behave," she commanded.

"I have the terrible feeling that the once-a-year schedule was no joke." He dried another dish.

"I never lie." She rinsed the silverware.

Philosphically he reminded himself, "But it did last twenty-four hours. I was just a little late getting back here. If I hadn't left in the first place I could have taken full advantage of your day."

She looked up at him and smiled. "You are simply fabulous."

"Really? What do you like best about me?" He tilted his head back and smiled just a little as he waited for the sugared words.

"You're a great writer," she began.

"Oh?" That was not what he had expected to hear. "What else?"

"You have a great sense of humor." She finished washing the skillet.

Somewhat impatiently he prompted, "What else?"

"You make good sandwiches and superb omelets," she enumerated his talents.

"I may strangle it out of you. What else?"

"Uh...."

"What about my lovemaking?" He looked supremely confident as he waited for her reply.

"What lovemaking?" She made her eyes as wide and as blank as she could.

"You didn't even notice?"

Lynn looked back down at the sink, spraying out the last of the soapsuds. "Did I miss something?"

"The kiss of forgetfulness!" He slapped his hand to his forehead. "I just gave it automatically. Damn. Now I'll just have to go through the whole interminable routine again so you can tell me how good I am."

With a sigh of long-suffering, Kevin took her hand and led her into the living room. "This is really a drag," he complained as he led her to the sofa and pulled her down next to him. "What do you remember about sex? I have to have some sort of framework before I can tell where to begin."

"'Sex'?" she asked obtusely.

"I always forget how potent that kiss can be to a susceptible woman." He aimed his eyelashes at the ceiling, thinking. "Now just where should I begin?" he asked rhetorically.

Lynn was helpful. "It is always best to begin—"

"At the beginning," he completed. "I know. My dear child—"

"I am older than you," she reminded him.

"Only in years, my child. In experience I far outdistance you."

"'Outdistance' me?" she questioned. "Do you want to race?"

"In a little while," he said agreeably. "We'll see how fast we can get from here to the bed. That's a fun thing to do. But in the meantime you need to know some basics."

She gave him her animated attention.

"It's about men and women. You are woman. I am man."

"Ah." She said that as if he had opened mental portals.

"Our bodies are made to lock together in an interesting, intricate way that is most enjoyable."

"How?" She tilted her head, willing to learn.

"The rubbing of bodies together causes a heat that is very pleasurable," he lectured. "Let's begin by taking off our clothes. They'll only get in the way of our lesson," he said in a tone that implied clothes were not important.

But she objected. "It's cold. There's a foot of snow on the ground." She waved a hand toward the windows.

"I could make a fire in the fireplace." He rose effortlessly from those entrapping sofa cushions and built the fire. Then he came back and sat beside her. "Let's see what's under your sweater," he suggested clinically.

She lifted it obediently and they both looked at her stomach. "Not very much," she said.

"Um. Let's lift it just a tad higher."

The bottoms of her breasts were exposed, and they examined these. She raised her eyes to his face and pronounced, "Lumps."

"Well, yes, but very nice lumps." He put one big,

warm hand on her stomach and smoothed that skin in slow strokes.

"I . . . like that." She judged with narrowed eyes.

"I do, too." He moved his hand up to the bottom of her "lumps" and pressed them, then took them fully into his hands to knead them and said, "I like this, too."

"It is rather interesting," she commented thoughtfully. She looked up at him to watch his face and he kissed her.

"That's called a 'kiss,'" he explained. "You have a fine natural ability there. Let's do it again."

"You can do it more than once?"

"Oh, yes," he assured her. "All you want."

She noticed that they did it a great deal. And when her clothes fell away to join his on the floor she was surprised. "When did you shed your clothes?"

He raised his head and asked, "Huh?" but then he deliberately lowered his whiskery face to slowly nudge along her tender skin. Goose bumps sprang upon her surfaces before a deeper sensation began to build inside her. A giddy thrill shot through her, causing her breasts to rise and making her gasp.

"You like that?"

She merely clutched his hair and curled her body and groaned.

"How about this?" He moved his hands slowly and his expression was calculating.

She drew in a long breath and writhed. "What time is the race?" she gasped.

"Pretty soon now," he promised.

"There's still a little time?" she questioned urgently.

"Only a little."

"Then...can I practice...on you?" she panted.

"I'm beginning to suspect that I failed to give you the kiss of for...aaaaaaaahhhhhhhhhh...." He gasped on a sharply indrawn breath.

"You like that?" she mimicked him.

"Yyyyeeeessssss." His hissed reply sounded like a steam blast.

"You're going to crush my skull," she admonished. "Loosen your grip a bit."

"Loosen yours," he moaned.

"Oh, sorry."

"That's okay. Help me up."

"You're already up." She stated the obvious.

"Help me to the bed," he begged.

She giggled as she stood up and tugged him to his feet. He took advantage of their upright position to hold her close down the length of his body and to kiss her yet again.

"On your mark..." she whispered. But she was standing against him, her arms clenched around his waist, her shoulders curled toward his body, relishing the feel of him.

He murmured, "Get set." But he picked her up and carried her into the bedroom and lay her on the bed. He leaned over her, and brought his head down to kiss her, holding his body off her with stiffened arms. "You are incredibly beautiful."

"So are you." She stroked his shoulders with selfish hands.

"Are you ready to see how this works?" he asked hoarsely.

"I think so," she whispered in distraction.

Lowering his body to hers, he showed her.

"So that's how it's done!" she breathed. "I'd have never figured it out just reading about it. How clever! Do you—" She went silent.

He paused and raised up on his elbows. "Do I what?"

Do you—" But she couldn't remember what, so she asked, "Do you kiss me?"

He did that. "Anything else?"

She frog-legged her feet up against the sides of his thighs and curled her body. After that she went a little crazy. Equally crazy were the sensations in her body—the thrills of desire being titillated and enhanced, then assuaged.

And when they lay panting and replete, she murmured, "I believe that could catch on. It's a form of exercise that should appeal to almost anyone."

He made a murmur of humor.

She propped herself up on one elbow. "Are you going to go back to sleep again?"

"I'm drained."

"But I gave you most of the steak last night."

"That was last night."

"I haven't had you but once since then! You should get more mileage out of a whole steak," she argued.

"You're expecting too much from one steak. You have no idea how voracious you are. An ordinary man could have been killed! I believe that first husband of yours didn't just divorce you, he ran for his life!"

She laughed. It was the first time she had found

anything even remotely funny about that long-ago abandonment. She ran her hand over his stomach and ruffled the mat of hair that textured it. "I didn't quite understand the whole process," she said, "and I think we should do it again more slowly. I got excited, and I've forgotten some of it."

"Later," he breathed, his eyes closed.

"But we're here in bed and undressed and we could just go about it so easily. It's convenient now, so why not?"

"I could never rise to the occasion."

She laughed dutifully and teased him. He grunted and groaned and protested, while she complained that he sure changed in a hurry. Why had he lost interest? He certainly had a short attention span. What kind of teacher was he, anyway, to give up so soon? She tousled his hair and rubbed his cheek and kissed his mouth, while he smiled a little and yawned and encouraged her to settle down. Finally he wrapped his arms around her, pulled her close, flung one leg over hers and trapped her there. He then went peacefully to sleep.

IT WAS ABOUT AN HOUR LATER on that wintry March morning when the phone rang. Lynn was startled to feel a bulk next to her in bed. For a minute she was disoriented and it scared her, before she remembered Kevin.

His voice gravelly, he suggested, "It's your phone. Maybe you'd better answer it."

She cleared her throat and blinked several times, although the value of blinking to help her sound alert was dubious. She picked up the phone and said, "Hello?"

It was the visiting nurse. "Lynn, there is no way I can make it over to see Mrs. Hobbs or Mr. Reed and they won't be getting their hot lunches today, either. Could you possibly check in on them? Or if you can't see them, can you contact someone else from your group? Everyone must be home today."

Not everyone was at his own home, Lynn thought, as she looked over at Kevin's marvelous form stretched out in her bed. His arms were folded behind his head, his lashes were on her and there was a faint smile on his lips. She returned her attention to the phone. "Sure. I'll be glad to."

"Remember, Mr. Reed grabs," the nurse warned.

"I'll remember." They spoke a bit more before hanging up.

"What are we 'glad to' do?" Kevin queried, suddenly wary.

"Just me," Lynn replied. "You don't have the equipment—"

"What's wrong with my equipment?" he challenged in mock indignation.

"To be out in this weather. I have to check on two housebound people."

He looked down his nose at her. "It just so happens that in the trunk of my car are boots, a heavy coat, rope, tool kit, tennis racket—"

"'Tennis racket'?"

"One showshoe." He seemed genuinely surprised that she hadn't figured that out. "And a snow shovel."

They went into the living room to look out the windows and watch the snow swirling around the house. It was not an inviting sight. "I will go," Lynn said bravely.

She went back into the bedroom and pulled on her long underwear. Kevin, too, dressed again, and as she headed for the kitchen, he took his coat from the rack and started to put it on.

"Where are you going?" She slid cans of soup and fruit from Kevin's stockpile into her coat pockets before pulling on her hat.

"I'm going to get my boots from the trunk of my car," he replied. "I'll come with you."

Lynn looked down at his dress shoes and said, "You can't. Why, you'll get snow in your shoes and freeze your feet! I'll get your boots for you."

He smiled at her and there was a pleased glint in his eyes that melted her insides together into a mess. She smiled back. Then she turned and floated down the stairs past the climbing people, but she had to struggle with the storm door. It opened outward, and there was snow against the bottom and ice under that.

However, Kevin materialized next to her and reached past her to shove the door open effortlessly. She appraised him and said flirtatiously, "The muscled Captain Force."

The wind whipped the snow around viciously as Lynn struggled to his car, where she had to work to get the key in the lock of the trunk. She finally had to take off her glove and put her bare hand against the keyhole long enough to melt the sliver of ice inside. This was not fun, but it worked.

She opened the trunk and snow blew into it. She fumbled and fought to get the boots, heavy gloves and a knitted helmet. If there was anything else he needed, he could get it himself after he had the boots. She slammed the trunk closed and struggled through the swirling snow, back to him. "To him." What a strange thing for her to think of—fighting her way back "to him."

She surged through the doorway with the wind and fell into his arms. It felt so good, and she laughed breathlessly. He continued holding her, watching her, and he said, "Your cheeks are red and your eyes look like sparkling sherry. Beautiful."

"It was the wind that reddened my cheeks. See? I didn't need a new diet or the sex."

"You're a wretched ingrate," he informed her.

"No, you're a con man. I'll bet you can think of dozens of reasons why I should make love with you."

Very tenderly he replied, "I can think of only one reason we should make love."

Her smile didn't reach her eyes. "Only one?"

But he was serious. "Do you want to know what it is?"

The smile dropped completely and she said, "No."

"You don't want to know the reason?" His expression was gentle.

"No." She turned away. Her whole body was still, and she felt something like fear.

He sat on the third stair and took off his shoes, knocked the snow out of the boots and pulled them on. He donned the woolen helmet and thrust his hands into the gloves. Then, breaking the silence, he said, "I can see now isn't the time to talk about it."

"No," she agreed quickly.

They went to see Mr. Reed first. As they stood in the lea of a house for a respite from the wind, she warned Kevin that Mr. Reed would rudely ignore him and try to grab her. Kevin didn't blame him. "If I had a choice between you and me, I'd try for you, too."

"They say it's part of senility."

"I've heard that." Kevin nodded.

She tilted a smile at him. "Then you're senile?"

"Not quite."

"Then what possible excuse can you have for always grabbing me?"

"I have to keep checking to be sure I haven't dreamed you." He grinned down at her, and then he said softly, "And there's the real reason."

"We'd better get going. I have cans of soup to fix for them and some oranges."

He shook his head once. "You're only delaying," he said, then took her hand and went first around the corner of the house, taking the brunt of the wind.

There were two other old men at Mr. Reed's house, and Mr. Reed didn't need either Kevin or the soup. He tried to get the others to go out into the hall because, he said, he needed to whisper something to Lynn. But Kevin took over, explaining that he'd finished three years of medical school and that he was almost as good as a nurse, and he'd be glad to help in any way. Mr. Reed didn't buy it. The other two old men chortled and wheezed and found it all hilarious. Lynn edged away, and Kevin ran interference between her and Mr. Reed until they could escape.

"Men!" Lynn exclaimed.

"How can you possibly be censorious of men after what you did to me?" Kevin accused primly.

She huffed and puffed and stuttered.

"I can see how guilt over your behavior has left you speechless. That will probably stay with you until another urge overwhelms you next year and you attack me again."

"You embarrass me," she said in a small voice, looking down, her face very serious.

"Oh, no!" he protested. "You shouldn't be embarrassed. It was beautiful! I'm so overwhelmed at your wanting me that I need to talk about it and brag and tease you about it. You won't allow me to be serious about you yet. I love you, Lynn."

"No!" She exploded. Again she said, "No!" She shook her head in denial. Then she turned away and struggled through the snow.

He caught her arm, but she tried to pull away from him. "Calm down, Lynn," he said. "We'll go carefully."

"Carefully"? Did he mean walking in the snowstorm—or did he mean with love?

They knocked and then used Lynn's emergency key to enter Mrs. Hobbs's tiny house. There was another stormbound old lady there, Mrs. Topper, and she was hovering over Mrs. Hobbs, who was lying on the bed, choking.

Kevin ripped off his coat as he went over to the bed. He murmured soft, calming words, telling Mrs. Hobbs what he was doing and why and what she should do. His hands moved her frail body as he turned her and helped her. Lynn and Mrs. Topper stood, their bodies tense, their hands clenched, their heads strained forward, concentrating on the struggle they were witnessing. And Kevin won.

When Mrs. Hobbs lay back, breathing, exhausted, Lynn brought Kevin a pan of warm water and a cloth. He wrung out the cloth and lay it on Mrs. Hobbs's throat to soothe it after the ordeal. And he gave her sips of tepid water to comfort her.

"That was a near thing. You should have let me go," she whispered hoarsely.

"So you're ready, are you?" He gently wiped her face with the warm cloth.

She nodded, looked sideways at Lynn and said, "I know Democrats are—" And all her wrinkles hunched up in humor.

"Don't laugh!" Lynn exclaimed in alarm.

"Not right now," Kevin also cautioned, but in a softer tone. Then he turned his head and coughed slightly. He asked Mrs. Hobbs's trapped visitor, "Will you be all right?"

"Fine." Mrs. Topper appeared quite capable.

Kevin told her, "We'll come back around supper-time."

"Don't worry about us" Mrs. Topper assured them.

"I'll be at Lynn's... for a time. After that, Lynn would know where to get in touch with me."

Mrs. Topper smiled knowingly. Lynn studied the ceiling, then remembered she was going to make some soup. She did that for the two old ladies, and Kevin fed Mrs. Hobbs. Being a natural flirt, Mrs. Hobbs enjoyed his attentions and smiled, even though she was dead tired. Then she slept.

With Kevin coughing, he and Lynn walked back to her apartment. They went inside, up the stairs and into the living room. Kevin still coughed. They took off their coats and hung them carefully in the shower, put their boots on a boot tray and peeled off some of their clothes. After the wind's buffeting, they were suddenly too warm indoors. Kevin coughed harder.

Lynn patted his back and asked, "Catching cold? You need some vitamin C." She went to get some for him, handed one tablet with a glass of orange juice and asked, "What would you like for—"

He coughed very hard. She felt his forehead and frowned at him, but he just shrugged and said, "It isn't a cold. I've caught Mrs. Hobbs. This is why I was asked to leave—" he went into a spasm of coughing "—medical school. I catch—" He coughed.

She praised him. "You were terrific."

He shook his head. "It happens every time."

"But you waited until after you saved her life." She paused while he coughed. Then she asked anxiously, "If she hadn't made it, you wouldn't have died on me, would you?"

"No, no. It's only empathy, not complete commitment."

"What can I do to counteract it?" she asked.

He just coughed.

"Bouillon! You gave her warm water to soothe her." She left Kevin in the rocking chair by the fire, coughing, and rushed to the kitchen to heat water. She went back to him, standing by him.

He smiled at her around his coughing and managed to gasp, "It's just...ridiculous."

She shouldn't have, but she couldn't stop her hand from going out and smoothing his hair, and she could not stop the tender words, "I think you're wonderful."

The teakettle whistled and she went back to the kitchen. She brought him the bouillon, then squatted to watch him sip it. It did soothe him. The coughing diminished and finally settled down and quit.

"It worked!" she crowed.

"Yeah," he sighed.

"So you gave up medicine and took up writing. Does it affect you when your characters get hurt or sick?"

"No," he replied. "It's only if I'm involved with someone having health problems."

"So you can zap a character's arm off and yours stays on?"

"Oh, yes," he assured her. "And when I wrote Westerns..."

"You wrote Westerns?" She was surprised.

"I started in Westerns. You know Kevin Walker isn't my real name?"

"What is it?"

"Terrance Maypole." He watched her face for response.

She considered it. "I like Terrance. That's a good name. So is Maypole. Why did you change it?"

"Terrance Maypole couldn't write *Apache Uprising*. There could be some question if the uprising concerned the maypole, right?"

"Very astute." She nodded, agreeing.

"Kevin Walker is my legal name now, so when we get married you'll be Mrs. Walker."

She snapped her head up and said, "I'm not getting married."

"Maybe not right away, but—"

"No! I will not be serious about this."

"This isn't serious?"

"No!" She was emphatic.

"You certainly fooled me."

"It was just...just...it was only...well, it was physical."

He agreed, his face pleasant and waiting.

"I mean, it wasn't...it isn't...it won't be...it's not...well, it's not serious."

"You just don't realize it yet," he told her complacently.

"I will not have you cluttering up my life. This is just a lark," she contended. "Fun...."

"I'll drink to that."

"We're just having an interlude," she explained carefully. "Because of the weather." She jerked a thumb toward the windows.

"'An interlude.'" He savored that. "Sounds interesting. Okay. We'll continue the interlude farce until you can face reality."

"Now, Kevin—"

"Now? Again? Honey, you ought to pace me a little better. I can't be hopping in and out of bed at this rate. You'll kill me."

"I meant—I didn't mean—" Her tongue stumbled and she blushed. Blushed! Thirty-two, and blushing!

"It's okay," he told her soothingly. "I've been asking around and everyone says you're free of any entanglement. I realize your life has been pretty bleak lately."

"It has not!" she protested. "You've been asking...what?"

"I just happened to inquire as to whether you were serious about anyone in particular," he explained.

"Who did you ask?" she queried.

"I have my sources, and I needed to know before I lost my heart to you."

"Kevin, I will not have any gossip and I will not have you moving in here or getting involved. I'm older than you, and I'm more experienced, and I can see how I've led you to believe I'm...interested."

"I should hope you are," he exclaimed. "If that's not 'interested,' I'd be terrified of 'interested'!" He grinned at her.

"I've been divorced by one man and I've been dumped by another. They were exactly like you—good-looking, charming and excessively attractive...."

"They couldn't have had my lower lip. You admitted that's unique."

"Or your eyelashes," she agreed.

"You said it was my lower lip!"

"Kevin, let's be serious for a minute."

"I am serious." He was suddenly earnest and sure. "You're the one who's avoiding being serious."

"Kevin," she admonished firmly.

He straightened his head, folded his hands together and gave her a bland look, but then he licked his lower lip and the corners of his mouth quirked insidiously.

"We cannot be serious—" she enunciated.

He raised his eyebrows.

"We cannot be serious about—"

"Now you are confusing me. First you tell me I have to be serious, and now you're telling me we can't be serious. What do you mean? I believe your mind has wandered and you badly need to be kissed.'' He rose and reached, but she backed away and screeched.

''If someone comes up here to see if you're being ravished, I'll leap up on the chandelier and convince them it was you after me!'' he scolded.

''I don't have a chandelier.'' She grabbed her hair with both hands.

''Sometimes you're very prosaic.'' He scowled at her. ''Are we beginning our first quarrel?''

She was a bit frantic, but she carefully lowered her hands, palms up, almost pleading. ''I am not trying to quarrel. I'm trying to tell you you have to be ser— You have to listen to me. *I am not going to become involved with you.*''

''What's the matter with me?'' he demanded indignantly. ''You like me, we work well together, you find my body acceptable, I'm willing to cook and clean—''

''I'm not opposed to having an affair,'' she said earnestly, ''but I will not get emotionally involved. Do you understand?''

''Just hanky-panky?'' He couldn't accept this and dismissed it. ''I can't ever recall hearing about a woman who wanted only an affair. They always want commitments. You Earth women are inconsistent.''

''If you want to have an affair, I'm perfectly willing. But I'll break off with you if you try to make it in any way permanent. Do you hear?'' she warned him.

He tilted his head forward and studied her as he tucked in that maddening lower lip.

She pushed for his reply. "Do you understand? Do you agree?"

He leaned his head back and continued to study her. Then he allowed his lip its freedom and probably deliberately let it protrude just a bit. It was shamelessly provocative. "We'll try it for a while and just see."

"We'll 'see' what?"

He smiled. "We'll just... 'see.'" He stretched out a hand invitingly and asked, "Shall we kiss on it?"

She wasn't sure she had made herself perfectly clear, or that perhaps, at this point, a handclasp would be smarter than a kiss. But there was that lower lip—waiting. She kissed him.

It was a captivating kiss, and Kevin showed his enjoyment with sounds of pleasure. He ran his hands down her back and cupped her bottom and pulled her close to prolong the moment. Then he said, "Soup won't be enough for lunch. I'm starved."

And he was. She had a duck in the freezer that she'd been avoiding and he got it out to thaw for dinner. She said doubtfully, "I've never baked a duck."

"It's a snap," he assured her. "Just leave everything to me."

"I don't particularly like duck." She was uncertain.

"We'll have an orange glaze. It'll be delicious."

"You won't be offended if I don't eat any?"

"You will. It'll be superb," he told her.

She wasn't convinced. "It's a good thing we aren't going to get involved. We're too different."

"We're different where it counts, being male and female, and we fit well where it does." He put the plastic-wrapped duck in cold water to thaw.

"That is true," she agreed. "We are good in bed."

"I was thinking of our humor and our imaginations." He gave her a sly, teasing look.

"Oh." She heated the soup while he made a stack of sandwiches, and they ate companionably but in silence. After they had cleared the table, they started washing dishes again.

Thoughtfully he said, "I know a lot about you. You're compassionate—you go out in a storm to see about other people, you can't destroy the artwork on the stairs because you want the artists to be able to come back and see their work.

"You have good friends." He watched his hands drying the dishes. "You're adorable with your nieces and nephews. You share openhandedly—like your steak and your woodpile. You care about other people. I love you...uh...that is—" he held up a staying hand "—I love you in the name of humanity. As in, 'peace and love'? You do remember that, don't you?"

"As much as I don't want to be hurt again," she said in all sincerity, "I don't want you hurt, either. It's as much for your protection as it is for mine. I know some very nice women. When our affair is over I'll help you find someone to love. That's the least a friend can do."

He froze as he asked, "You could turn me over to another woman?"

"Well...after our affair is over." She was appalled

by the feeling of devastation that swept through her at the very thought of turning him over to another woman. She was quiet as they finished the dishes, and she faced that strange, bleak feeling. She wondered why that should be? It must be that this taste of him was still a novelty. She was not ready to end their affair.

She would probably always be fond of him, she projected sentimentally, and he would be special to her because of their collaboration on his book. Of course, they'd collaborated deliciously in bed, too. That was the reason for this feeling of bereavement. She wasn't ready to do without the newly redis-covered rapture of sex.

She relaxed, reassured that everything was all right, and she asked Kevin, "What about the next book? And I don't mean the blank one with the pages mostly turned sideways."

He studied her as she dried her hands on his dish towel. Then he hung it up. Together they moved into the living room, where he sat on the sofa and she took the rocking chair. He began to outline the es-sence of the new book.

She listened and questioned him about characters and they settled down to work. She moved over to the typewriter while he told her where he thought the romance scenes could be. She asked him more questions and typed notes. Kevin paused and pre-pared the duck for the oven.

Later, as he was breathing deeply of the rich aroma of roasting duck, Lynn was opening windows and spraying Lysol around to counteract the smell.

"You need instruction in the finer things in life," Kevin observed.

"That stench is one of the finer things in life?"

"The aroma of roasting duck is one of the best," he confirmed.

"It stinks." She was positive. Then she brightened. "We are so different! I worried needlessly! By the time we're bored physically, we'll barely be courteous to each other."

"Do you think we'll ever become bored with each other?"

"Undoubtedly," she replied cheerily. "We're world's apart."

"Anything too sweet is cloying," he reminded her. "Opposites attract."

"We could never live together." She babbled on in her relief. "The smell of your cooking would drive me out. You probably like Limburger cheese."

"It's delicious," he agreed.

At that she threw out her arms as if freed of shackles and laughed. "It'll never happen! We can just have fun and enjoy it while it lasts!" Going over to him, she pushed his unresisting body over on the sofa, lay on top of him and kissed him.

But when she looked into Kevin's face she had the odd feeling she was witnessing the look of a fox who wasn't hungry as it watched a mouse frolicking, unafraid. Ridiculing her own thoughts, she kissed him again. And the deliciousness of the kiss blotted out that little niggling insight.

12

IT WAS IN THE MIDDLE OF THE NIGHT when the phone rang and Mrs. Topper's quavering voice asked, "Lynn, can you reach that nice young man? We need him!"

"Is it Mrs. Hobbs?" Lynn asked quickly.

"Oh, yes," Mrs. Topper urged. "And it's bad."

"We'll be right there." Lynn hung up and turned over, but Kevin was already getting out of bed and reaching for his clothes. She threw back the covers to get up.

"Go back to sleep," he said gently in his deep voice. "I know the way, and there's no reason for you to go out in this weather."

"No," she replied briskly. "You may need me."

"She was all right last night when we went back and checked on her. It'll be okay."

"I'll go, too." She was determined.

"Do you have a flashlight?"

"Yes."

They hurried. The wind still whipped over the ice, and it was very cold. They wrapped scarves around their woolen helmets and struggled through the frozen night.

Mrs. Hobbs knew them. She held up a hand. Did she mean to greet them? Or did she mean to fend off their help? Kevin didn't even get his coat off, but he had her in his hands when she laughed a gurgle and died in his arms.

He and Lynn cleaned her and put a fresh gown on her and changed the bed. Mrs. Topper wept tears that rolled slowly down her lined cheeks, and Lynn, too, sniffled. So did Kevin. Lynn asked him, "Why are you crying? You hardly knew her. She was very old, and she said she was ready."

"I'm emotionally involved with you," he replied simply.

She gave him a stark, scared look because of the wave of pleasure that went through her chest at his words.

He hastened to amend his words. "You're unhappy, so I am. You know how I am."

She nodded tersely and tied up the soiled sheets. Mrs. Topper said she would wash them, so Lynn carried them to the laundry room. Before she helped Mrs. Topper back into bed, Lynn sat with her over a warm glass of milk. Then she went back to Kevin. With no need to discuss it, they settled in to share the wake. The lovers silently dusted and straightened the little house before Lynn made them some tea. As she sipped hers she walked around, running her hands over the familiar treasures that Mrs. Hobbs had loved. Lynn leaked tears, and she saw that Kevin's eyelashes were wet, too. "You're a dreadful softy," she said, and kissed his cheek.

He coughed discreetly and replied, "Not really. I knew it would capture your attention and you'd go mushy and be sweet to me."

"I wish Mrs. Hobbs could have known you better," Lynn said tenderly. "She would have loved you."

"You obviously loved her," he said gently, touching her with comforting tenderness.

"She enjoyed life so much." Lynn paused pensively. "Did you hear her as she died? She laughed."

"That was the death rattle." He said it easily, for his view of death was more realistic than most.

"She laughed," Lynn insisted stubbornly. "She probably saw all her dead husbands and lovers fighting to see who would greet her first."

"Is that why you're having an affair with me?" he asked. "You want me hanging around the River Styx, waiting to greet you when you cross? Waiting there with the rest of your husbands and lovers?"

"Neither my husband nor Mark would wait for me," she said, accepting the fact.

"I would," he promised in a husky voice.

"Don't start that," she chided, but her voice was soft. She looked around, a little melancholy. "I wish Mrs. Hobbs could have lived just a little longer and given me the secret. She relished life through everything."

"Don't you?" he asked quietly. "Don't you relish life?"

"Not all the time." She sat in a rocker in the small living room, and he sprawled uncomfortably on an old, curlicued, walnut sofa upholstered with horsehair.

His tone was serious but comforting. "You need to make some changes in your thinking. If you can get out of bed in the morning and walk, and if you can eat and digest your breakfast, you're well-off."

She considered his words before she said, "That's a good way of putting it. Maybe I don't appreciate what I have. I only think of what I haven't got."

"Refocus," he advised.

She viewed him with a fond smile. "For such a young man, you're really very wise."

"Good Lord, I'm only about two and a half years younger than you, old lady."

"Two and a half years is a large gap between a woman and a man. You won't catch up with me for thirty years," she replied stiffly.

"It'll be worth the wait." His tone was exaggeratedly male and rather indulgent.

"Now, Kevin—"

"I love you, you knucklehead."

"I've told you—" she warned.

"And I've told you. You need to adjust to it. Mature people can, you know." Then he dismissed the subject and to distract Lynn from her grief he went on to talk about an Irish wake he went to once. And he declared that the wildest times of all, and two things that everyone must experience, were German weddings and Irish wakes.

"The particular Irish wake I attended happened quite by chance. I was visiting a friend and went with him to the wake. It was in the country and the 'viewing' was, of course, at the family house. Someone stole the corpse and sat it in the emergency outhouse. The grieving wife wasn't very understanding."

"I should think not!"

"She got mad and called the police," Kevin remembered. "She thought Mick should be back in his coffin."

"How could they have done that to that poor woman?" Lynn shook her head in disgust.

"The police felt the same way. They were German and Germans are great at a German wedding, but they aren't any good at an Irish wake. Anyway, they took about half of us down to the station."

"Of...us?" Her eyes darted to his.

He ignored that. "Fortunately the sergeant was an Irishman, and we sat around exchanging interesting stories until the rest were reasonably sober and able to attend the funeral."

"I can't believe you'd be involved in something like that."

"At the time it all made good sense."

Then Lynn talked about Mrs. Hobbs. How she'd had a really tough life on the surface of it, but she'd enjoyed every minute. She'd wanted five more lifetimes, or was it four more? Lynn couldn't remember. And Lynn looked through the doorway to the bed where Mrs. Hobbs lay so strangely quiet, and she was swamped with grief.

Kevin came to her, lifted her from her chair and sat down on the rocker. With her on his lap, he consoled her. Lynn didn't feel the least self-conscious about Kevin holding her and giving her sweet kisses because she knew Mrs. Hobbs would understand. Then she thought about whistling under the window and never again seeing the drape waggle, and her grief freshened.

During the night the wind died, too. The snow-plows began laboring to return Fort Wayne to working order, and Lynn and Kevin helped with all the ramifications of the funeral. There weren't many people to contact. There was a granddaughter working in Saudi Arabia who couldn't come in time, and there was a grandson whose wife was in labor and he couldn't leave her. But he asked if Lynn would arrange a visitation for Mrs. Hobbs's nearby kin, the neighbors and her telephone friends. She agreed.

A cousin showed up early with a truck and simply took the horsehair sofa. Kevin called the grandson, who said it was all right, but after that they held down the Hobbs's fort, deterring any bold visitors who wanted to carry off what they called "momentos."

Kevin was especially good at thwarting what amounted to thievery; he was so relentlessly tactful. Then, he was also rather large and he was very sure he was in the right. He took down names and listed what Mrs. Hobbs had allegedly promised, explaining that either the object would be mentioned in Mrs. Hobbs's will or the grandchildren would decide how things were to be divided.

Lynn watched him dealing with the determined scavengers, and she noted that he always got his way. He was charming and gentle about it, but he did get his own way. He only appeared to be a civilized and urbane Terrance Maypole. It was a facade.

There was a disturbing thought growing in Lynn's mind. Kevin was doing it to her, too. He had insinu-

ated himself into her life and into her bed, and that
was exactly what he'd set out to do.

Lynn suddenly had a very clear picture of Kevin
at the Irish wake. She bet he'd been the inciter in the
purloining of the Mick's body.

He was a leader. He only made people think
they'd consented. Look at the sexual state he'd excited in her—he was an exciter-inciter. He'd got her
so overwrought that she'd attacked him at the front
door and would have had him right there on the
floor if he hadn't picked her up and carried her to
the bed.

How devious he was. He had actually accused her
of being sexually wild and it was he. He was very
dangerous. Just look at the lives he was interfering
with right here among Mrs. Hobbs's hapless handful of relations and acquaintances.

Ah...how she would miss Mrs. Hobbs. Lynn
wondered how long it would be before she would
jog on by and not stop to whistle under the window.
Her eyes moved over to Bud Turner just as he looked
up, and their eyes caught in mutual understanding.
How often would Bud think to whistle at the window? And Lynn smiled to remember how flirtatious
Mrs. Hobbs had always waved to Bud but only waggled the drape for her.

One of the old ladies paying her respects crept
over to Lynn and smiled as she commented about
"That nice boy," meaning Kevin.

"Where did you meet Kevin?" Lynn inquired politely.

"Over at the ice-cream place on Rudisil. Just before the ice storm. We were sitting in those little chairs listening to the weather report on the radio as we ate our ice cream. He had almond praline. I remember that because we talked about it. I was surprised he didn't have chocolate. Most boys have chocolate, you know. But he had almond praline. I had chocolate." She smiled, showing her too-perfect teeth.

They were joined by a lovely, leggy blonde who had long hair and a perfectly stunning body. "She's Lanie, from down the road," the old lady informed Lynn. "It's really Melanie, but everyone calls her 'Lanie.'" Then she said to Lanie, "I was just telling her about that nice young man. I met him over at the ice-cream place on Rudisil, by the bookstore there on Calhoun. You know the place?"

And Lanie said, "Kevin? I used to go with him." She smiled across the room, where Kevin was talking to someone else, and then she added, "He's so sweet."

Lynn went speechless with absolute fury. How dared that blond biddy say Kevin was "sweet"? Lynn didn't hear any more of the conversation but concentrated on being calm and indifferent that any piece of fluff would coo over Kevin. No man wanted his name bandied about that way!

And Lynn instantly recognized her temper was really a protective feeling toward her...collaborator. Thank heaven it wasn't anything as dumb as jealousy, and it was a good thing it was simply a sense of proper conduct.

That Lanie was trash. She had brought over a delicious stew, probably from Hall's Deli, and she was being very helpful in order to draw attention to herself. How obvious!

So Lynn was stiff and hostile until Lanie said she had to run home because it was time to nurse her new baby. With that revelation, Lynn's fury dampened to only coolness. Nevertheless she was glad when Lanie left.

A death made one think of life, Lynn discovered, and as the day went on she sorted out all the things she was grateful for in her life. She apologized to God for being so crabby and for not appreciating all the pluses in her life. She named them... and Kevin was one.

Then she debated with herself just what she ought to do about him. If she ever did want a permanent relationship she would consider one with Kevin, she admitted that, but she did not want one. Then she discovered herself dreaming of living with him and having his babies. Thinking of what beautiful children he would have....

SEVERAL DAYS LATER, Kevin came by with the first hundred pages of the new book. As he talked about it, Lynn studied him. The way he moved and spoke transfixed her. God would have to be pleased with the way he'd turned out.

She watched as he gestured, and she thought his hands were beautiful. So expressive. Then she thought of those hands moving on her, thrilling her. She gazed at his lower lip and felt an intense longing to kiss him, to feel his mouth on her, to touch it with her tongue.... And as her eyes took in his relaxed body, she remembered it tense and hard against her, over her, in her.

She stood up and pulled her sweater off over her head. He stopped talking. Efficiently she slid her trousers off her hips, down her legs and kicked them aside as she hooked her thumbs into her panties. She looked up to see Kevin watching her, startled and speechless except to ask, "What are you doing?"

She grinned at him and replied, "It's your lower lip. You've been waggling it at me in a perfectly lascivious way and I cannot resist. I must have it. And I suppose I'll have to have the rest of you, too."

"How do you know I want to make love right this minute?"

Standing there like *September Morn*, with her panties down over her hips, she paused and looked at him. "Oh," she said blankly. Then she shrugged. "I thought you were always ready."

"Not necessarily," he replied.

She hesitated, then pulled her panties back up and reached for her sweater and began to turn it right side out.

"What are you doing?" he asked again.

It had to be obvious what she was doing, she thought, but explained clearly, "I'm putting my clothes back on." And she pulled the sweater over her head and jerked it down.

"Why?" He sounded indignant.

"You said no." She was explicit.

"Well, what the hell if I did? Aren't you going to argue? I just mentioned that I wasn't always ready. I didn't say I didn't want to, or that I couldn't be convinced. Why can't you cajole? Sweet-talk?''

She was cool now, and she replied, "You sounded sure. You didn't say, 'Nooo.' You said, 'No.'"

"It's a damned good thing you're a woman." He was exasperated. "You'd make a lousy man. If women said, 'How about it?' and men said, 'No,' and the women just gave up, what would happen to the human race? You have to work at love. No man worth his salt would just ask and give up with the first no."

"What if she really didn't want to?" Lynn snapped.

"There's a third no," he explained.

"You said, 'No.'" She turned her trousers right side out, shook them out and flipped them out straight to put them on.

He lunged off the sofa with no trouble and stopped her. He pulled her down backward and sat her on his lap. Then he sighed in irritation. She sat straight and stiff, looking at him out of the corners of her eyes. Her chin was up and her lips were set in a thin line.

He had one hand clamped across her thighs to prevent her escape, and he put the other hand to his forehead and groaned, "It is just hell always having to be the one to train a woman."

"How many have you trained?" she inquired in a parsimonious voice that intended to quarrel.

"I've never trained any," he admitted candidly. "But men talk and complain about it to such an extent that we novices never realize there are any untrained women left. From all accounts, training one

is the pits. Now be quiet while I try to remember
how to begin."

"'Novice'?" she spat. "At Mrs. Hobbs's funeral
there was a blonde with long hair who said she'd
gone with you and that you're 'sweet'!"

"Oh. Yeah. That was Lanie," he said. "Her mother
read *Gone With The Wind* any number of times and
figured a girl named 'Melanie' would be proper and
precious."

"Just how 'sweet' were you?" Lynn demanded
through her teeth.

"That rankle a little?" He smiled.

"No, of course not. It's none of my affair." She
tried to move off his lap, but he pulled her back and
clamped her rigid body against him.

She twisted her head around and gave him a
penetratingly cold stare and said deliberately, "No."

He laughed. Then he kissed the side of her neck
and blew into it and sent a shiver down her spine.

She squirmed and wiggled and objected.

"If you don't sit still and allow me to train you
properly, I can't vouch for my restraint. I would hate
to rush the training. I understand if it isn't done
properly, it's a lot like trying to travel on a half-
broken horse."

"Are you comparing me...to...to..." she sputtered. She was all curled up, her arms folded over
her chest, while his were locked around them, holding her captive.

"That was a poor analogy," he soothed her. "Now
let's see if I can recall the words of the great lover,
William Hardin. I do wish I had more contact with

him. A master. But hearing a few words from a brilliant man is worth reams of drivel from those who are only competent."

A giggle threatened, but Lynn subdued it. "Was William Hardin a real man?"

"Oh, yes! I only wish he had time to be my mentor."

"Is he still alive?"

"Alive and probably seducing that lucky woman...slowly."

"'That woman'?"

"He's monogamous," Kevin explained. "More's the pity. Someone like him should be spread around. Savored by more than one selfish woman." He shook his head sadly as he sighed.

Her giggle almost escaped.

"He always begins with a wink," Kevin told her. "He has a catalog of winks." He shifted her a little on his lap. "Now pay attention. I'll wink hello. Then I'll wink that I think you're cute. Then I'll wink saying I want to be with you, and finally I'll wink a well-done. Watch."

Biting her lower lip so as not to appear too amused by him, she could not resist watching. She looked at his eyelashes and waited.

"Can you see the nuances?" He smiled somewhat cockily.

"You already did them?" She was surprised.

"Weren't you paying attention?" He frowned at her.

"You're through?" She frowned back.

"I'm not good at retakes," he complained. "I guess

I was too subtle for you. Watch now." He opened his eyelashes so that she could actually glimpse the warm gray irises, and he blatantly winked.

Lynn pretended to faint.

"Damn," he said softly as if to himself. "Hardin warned us about just such a thing. We never really understand our own power."

Lynn's laughter bubbled inside her and she had to clamp her lips tightly to keep it from escaping. But the faint had necessitated her complete relaxation and Kevin had taken full advantage of that, arranging her body to suit himself. After he'd peeled off her sweater, he lay her flat.

Continuing the pretense, she "came to" and looked down her chest to where Kevin was grazing along her breasts. "What are you doing?" she inquired.

"This is Martian mouth-to-mouth," he said.

"Martian women breathe through their breasts?" That was difficult to believe.

"That's why they have such big ones," he postulated. "Sorry about knocking you over with my wink. I didn't mean to."

"It's probably just as well you have those eyelashes. They screen women from the potency of your winks. A safety valve."

"Do you think so?" He was pleased.

She nodded positively.

"I can see that your training period is going to be extensive. It may well take years." He sounded as though he were telling her she'd have to wear braces on her teeth.

"How can you tell if I'm trainable?"

"You're a challenge." He was brave about it. "You've been allowed to go too long without the proper guidance. You don't know all the moves...."

So of course, minutely and very briefly, Lynn had to move in a titillating way. His lips parted, and he inhaled in a rush.

"How was that?" she asked innocently.

"You—" He coughed. "You...show...some... promise." He sat up and pulled her after him, holding her across his chest. He kissed her earnestly—no nonsense and concentrating on it.

She pushed a hand between them and fought the buttons on his shirt. Dragging the material open, she pressed her breasts against his bare chest as his kiss went on.

Her arms went up around his shoulders and back; her hands fingered him; her body squirmed against him; her teeth nibbled at his lower lip—which belonged to her—she hummed and sighed and her body moved. And while her hands were smoothing, her knees rubbed together and her toes were curling.

He raised his mouth a fraction as he growled, "You been reading ahead?"

Pouting her lips so they would touch his, she replied, "Only the answers in the back of the book— the chapter quizzes."

"Well, I suppose the only smart thing to do is to check you out on what you think you know." He sighed as if dreading it.

"A pop quiz?" she asked excitedly.

"Yes." He dragged the word out.

She struggled unsuccessfully to sit up as she began, "The zones of—"

"Show me!" His voice had become very tight.

"I thought I was supposed to use a chart." She turned to him.

"Use me," he commanded.

"Do you mind that terribly?" She sat there, naked on his lap, and smiled as she raised her hands to comb her tousled hair.

"No." His voice was intense and he was watching her avidly. He repeated urgently, "Use me."

"Would you mind taking off your clothes?"

"No." He lifted her aside, leaned over and pulled off his shoes and socks. Then he stood, undid his trousers and slid out of them and his shorts.

Lynn was sitting on her heels on the sofa, her hands folded demurely on her lap, watching him with a faint smile. She reached out and stroked one hand down his naked hip and watched his body react. "You're supposed to be aloof."

"I am," he lied.

"You don't look it."

"Believe me," he grated. "I'm aloof."

She laughed as she lightly ran her hands over her own thighs.

He stretched, reaching out his arms and spreading his legs like Leonardo's *Man in a Circle*. She straightened to her knees and began to lecture, touching his erogenous zone to illustrate.

He didn't have any zones that didn't arouse him. Disbelieving, she slowly bent over and touched his ankle. It was not immune. Then she reached up and felt his elbow, and she taunted, "You're too easy!"

"I am not!"

"I think you'd react even to my being touched."

He gave her a wary look.

So she sat up on the back of the sofa and lifted her knee and smoothed her hand up her ankle as she smiled at him, and he did react. Then she straightened her back and ran her hand up her forearm and past her elbow, but he walked around the sofa and scooped her from it and carried her into the bedroom.

"I'm not finished," she protested.

"I almost am." He dropped her in a bounce on the bed and went after her.

She laughed in her throat, and he growled in his as he tumbled her around and drove her into a passionate frenzy. But then he slowed down and made love to her.

Later, as she lay against his chest, she murmured, "William Hardin would be proud of you."

She sensed him smiling.

"You're so empathetic, when you thrill me and I'm writhing with pleasure, are you thrilled in turn?"

"I don't believe my being thrilled by you is empathy."

WHEN HE CAME THE NEXT DAY, he brought a suitcase. She held the street door and stood in his way as she asked sharply, "What are you doing with that?"

He smiled and said easily, "I just brought a clean shirt and some things."

"Oh, no you don't!" she objected. "You're not going to move in here."

He looked blank. Then he said reasonably, "Let me in. We can argue better inside. If I stand out here with a suitcase and we shout at each other, your neighbors might notice."

Without thinking, she stepped back, and he got inside. She was tight-lipped and her body trembled. She said, "I'm not going to live here with your things—and occasionally you—and worry that my mother will look in the closet or into a drawer and see something obviously masculine and know!"

"You're thirty-two years old," he argued. "If you want to live with me that's your business."

"Not in my family, it isn't! I had a cousin who tried that. His bathrobe was hanging in the back of her closet, but my aunt found it!"

'The old snoop," Kevin commented mildly.

"And the whole family was like a flock of ravens. That poor girl. She had to marry him!" Lynn reported, still shocked.

"Really?" He grinned.

"It isn't funny!" she chastised. "They have two kids already!"

"Isn't she happy?" he asked.

She hesitated. "That's beside the point!"

"But she is happy?" He persisted.

"Her's was the eighteen-month-old."

"Our princess?" He was delighted.

"No, the little redhead."

Kevin smiled very tenderly. "I'd like a little princess."

"Never." She rejected the whole package with the automatic response. "Not with me. I've told you all along this is only a brief affair." And she knew she lied. Her eyes sought his with that sudden knowledge.

"How brief an affair?" he probed.

"For a while." She was evasive, and her eyes moved aside to avoid his seeing she was not being truthful.

"This month?"

She could feel the sting of beginning tears. She examined her fingers.

"Next month?" he asked softly.

Her insides squirmed in misery, but she managed to shrug as if it didn't matter to her.

He put a tender hand on her shoulder and reminded her heartlessly, "And then you'll find me one of your friends to marry?"

Her lips parted in a gasp and her miserable eyes looked up into his. "Not...right away."

"Could you?"

"Now?" She was appalled by the thought.

"No, Lynn. Could you really turn me over to another woman?"

"I...." She was slowly shaking her head. She looked up, her heart faltering, her whole body wanting to moan in despair. "I...." She tried again.

"You what?" he coaxed with a strange tenderness that almost wrecked her.

"I'm not through with you yet." Her eyes were fixed on his lashes.

"Will you let me know when you are?"

She nodded minutely, her body yearning for him. Her soul was in some sort of dreadful torment. She felt awful.

He picked up his suitcase and kissed her cheek. "I'll be in touch." And he left.

13

SHE DIDN'T HEAR FROM HIM for three days. Then he called. "Kevin?" she squeaked.

"Hi." His voice was solemn.

"Hi," she replied. Then there was a silence.

"How are the plants?"

"Oh." She looked around. "Okay."

After a pause he asked, "How's the writing?"

"Slow." Who could concentrate on writing when all she thought of was Kevin?

"How are you?" His voice was very intimate in her ear.

"I've missed you," she admitted.

"Are you telling me I'm finally getting to you?"

"I'm not sure it's emotional." She tried that tack. "But I have missed you."

He sighed in her ear. "It's a start." There was another silence.

"Can you come over?"

"Want me to?" There was a note of caution in his tone.

"Please."

"Why?"

She hesitated, unsure of herself. "Well, I just...it's just that...I'd like to see you."

"I'm at my cousin's house in Huntington, so I'll be here in twenty minutes," he promised.

But it took him twenty-two. She opened the street door and it was like the first time. The look they exchanged was that clear, that weighing. It was as if scales of blindness had fallen away. Lynn had been so bent on searching for flaws that she'd been blinded to him. Now she saw Kevin, the real man, and she looked at him with her heart in her eyes.

He smiled just a little and reached out and touched her hair. "You're letting your hair grow!"

Of course it had been gradual, but hadn't he noticed it until now? She moved her body and her head in a rather elaborate pattern of contrived indifference. "You said once...." She was flooded with the knowledge of her love for Kevin, and it was so overwhelming that she didn't know what to do.

He continued to smile down at her. "I said what?"

A little breathlessly she revealed, "That you like long hair, and I just thought...."

"You mean I'm going to be tolerated long enough to see it long?" His deep voice was tender.

Lynn peeked at his lashes. "Maybe."

"'Maybe'! I could throttle you. Kiss me nicely and tell me again that you missed me."

She finally became aware that she was freezing in the doorway and said, "Come in."

"I get to actually come inside?" He pretended elaborate surprise.

"Don't be impossible." She moved back for him and then closed the door.

They started up the stairs, passing the string of

climbing people who never made it, and they went
into her apartment, where she closed the door and
shivered, rubbing her own shoulders. He took off
his coat and wrapped it around her, and the heat of
his body, captured there in the fleece lining, almost
melted her. Then he held the collar of the coat in his
big hands and pulled her to him.

His voice low, he demanded, "Tell me you missed
me."

"Um." She had him there with her, so she could
tease.

"Tell me you've been out of your mind with
wanting me here."

She batted her lashes at him, smiled secretively
and said, "Perhaps."

"Tell me you love me madly and your body is
starving for mine."

She chuckled indulgently. "Men!"

"What's wrong with us?" he asked.

"Men are just impossible." She shook her head.
"You can't live with them, and you can't live without them."

"That's about women," he said. "And you do like
men...and me. You like me!"

"Uh...." She pretended to study him, deciding.

"You do, too!" He was indignant.

She kissed him. She flung her arms around his
neck and she leaned against him and she really
kissed him. And he accepted that with great good
will.

She began to steam inside that great coat, whose
fleece was now heated by her body as well as his

She broke from his grasping hands and shook the coat off. Then he hastened to hang it up and get rid of the damned thing. When he took her back into his arms and kissed her to a fare-thee-well, it occurred to Lynn that there must be something shockingly erotic about that doorway that encouraged reckless, steamy embraces.

He lifted his mouth so they could breathe like long-distance runners and he gasped, "Are your secret places quivering yet?"

"Are yours?" she countered.

"Obviously."

"You deliberately set out to arouse me," she accused him.

"I fight dirty," he agreed. "All's fair, you know."

Without having remembered moving, she found them trapped in the cushions on the sofa. Her shirt was unbuttoned and her hands were up under his sweater; they were locked in a serious entanglement. And then the doorbell buzzed.

Nose to nose they stared at each other, and she knew he was remembering this very same thing happening once before, because he growled, "Um." Ordinarily that was a nice sound, but this time it sounded like a dog's serious warning.

They untangled, and she went to the window. She opened it and yelled down, "Who is it?"

"Hello, Lynn," a male voice called up. "It's Mark Blackwood."

Lynn turned in shock and stared at Kevin, who had frozen at the name and looked completely blank. Lynn shrugged elaborately and yelled, "Just a minute." She closed the window and hurriedly buttoned her shirt, unzipped her trousers, carefully tucked in her shirttail, rezipped, pulled her collar straight, went to the mirror, finger-combed her hair—and thought she looked just as if she had been tumbled in a haystack.

"That's the guy who dumped you?" Kevin's voice was intense.

"Yeah." She ran to the kitchen and put a tea towel under the faucet, wrung it out and lay it briefly on her face. She came back into the living room and looked at Kevin, who was still just standing there. "Am I okay?" she asked distractedly.

And then he began to smile. His eyes crinkled and he nodded. She took a deep breath, straightened her back, put her chin up and walked firmly to the door and opened it. She gave Kevin a last minute once-over and hissed, "Straighten your sweater," before she went down the stairs.

She opened the street door and stood back with a slight, polite smile as she said, "Hello, Mark." He was exactly as he'd always been, with a big, beautiful smile on his handsome face, and it meant absolutely nothing to her. He was only a man. An ordinary man. Then she looked around him. "Is Karen with you?"

"No. We're separated," he said dismissively as he moved inside and closed the door. "You've cut your hair!"

She gave her hair a forward and backward sweep and said, "Oh, yes. It was a nice change."

He put a hand up and just almost touched her

hair, as if he was restraining himself, and he smiled at her tenderly. "It's very attractive."

She said an automatic, "Thank you," and led the way up the stairs. How strange. Here was Mark for whom she grieved, and she felt nothing. He was a complete zero.

"How've you been?" he asked.

"Fine," she replied, and she gave him a measured look. No two men were alike. It wasn't "men" who had hurt her. It was only two men: Steve and then Mark. Neither came even close to being Kevin.

Mark paused on the stairs, remembering the different climbing figures. "I've thought of them so many times. And...I've thought about you, Lynn," he said in his deep husky voice. "I made a terrible mistake."

She didn't reply. They had reached the living room and she looked to where Kevin was supposed to be, but he wasn't there. The door to the bedroom was closed. What was he up to? Giving her privacy? Now how was she going to get him back into the living room without going over and knocking on the bedroom door? Why couldn't he have just stayed put?

Men tended to be totally idiotic. There was no earthly reason for her to be alone with Mark. If she had wanted Kevin out of sight in the bedroom, she would have told him so. Or sent him out the back door. "Would you like some coffee?" she offered Mark formally, wondering how soon she could get rid of him.

"Please." He took off his coat and put it on the

coatrack. "Remember when we bought that? That was a fabulous day."

She turned at the kitchen door and said blankly, "The coatrack?"

"Yes. We went to that auction out near Columbia City. Don't you remember?" Mark appeared surprised.

"Oh...yes." But it had to be apparent she didn't remember anything about it. She was such a dreadful liar. "Sit down." She went through the kitchen door. "I'll just be a minute."

But he strolled over to the front windows and looked down. "I've thought about your little nest up here so often."

From the kitchen she asked, "Where did you and Karen live?"

"I don't want to talk about Karen," he replied petulantly.

"Are you back in Fort Wayne permanently?" She tried that.

"Yes," he agreed. "To mend my life and have it go as it was supposed to."

She returned to the living room, ready to go and open the bedroom door to yank Kevin out of there, when, as if on cue, the door clicked open and a bare-chested, tousled Kevin stood sleepily in the doorway, buckling his belt. He yawned and scratched his hairy chest as he peered out and asked, "Company?"

The two in the living room could see that the bed behind him was rumpled and the blanket trailed down to the floor.

Lynn watched him, wondering what in the world to expect. He scooped up his sweater and padded barefoot into the living room. Standing there before the entranced pair, he stretched his muscular body leisurely. Then he pulled the sweater lazily over his head and grinned at them. "Do I smell coffee?" he inquired of Lynn before telling Mark, "I'm more alert after I have my coffee." He implied he had just got up.

Lynn introduced the two men, who guardedly shook hands. Then Kevin sprawled on the sofa, leaving Mark with the choices of sharing the sofa with Kevin, sitting on one of the straight chairs by the processor or using the rocking chair. He chose the rocker, and on that homey seat he sat, stiff and unbending. Scowling. And silent.

In contrast Kevin was relaxed, friendly and grinning. Lynn mostly chewed on her lip as she sat by Kevin on the sofa. *One should never underestimate a writer,* she thought. But, then she was a writer, and it would never have occurred to her to make a caller of Kevin's think they were having an affair. What a wicked prank! Of course, Mark was not her boyfriend. What mischief was Kevin up to?

Kevin carried the conversation. He discussed the progress in the basketball tournaments, he talked about the weather and he mentioned he and Lynn were collaborating on a love story. He put a world of meaning in those last two words as he turned and gave Lynn a possessive look.

Mark's replies were short grunts. When Lynn served the coffee, he ignored Kevin and tried to exclude him from a conversation with her. Kevin intruded. Finally Mark snapped at Lynn, "Is he living here with you?"

"Yes," Kevin said.

"No," Lynn said.

And Kevin raised his eyebrows and grinned, then said quickly, "No. No, I'm not." And he laughed.

Lynn shot him an astonished look, and he was very amused.

Mark was not. "When could I see you alone?" he asked Lynn. "We have a lot to talk about."

"Well..." began Lynn.

"What's on the calendar, honey?" Kevin asked. "Don't I have a Fine Arts meeting next Tuesday? You could see him then. I probably won't be free until—oh, nine-thirty or maybe even ten o'clock. You'd have the time for a nice chat."

"Kevin," she warned him. "You are not living here." There! Let him wiggle out of that!

He quickly made his face serious and said to Mark, "I am not living here." Then he grinned as if he had accomplished a task in the telling.

Now who would believe him? Lynn managed to frown at him, but just barely.

Mark rose and took Lynn's hand. As she struggled to get up from the sofa, Kevin helpfully gave her bottom a boost. Mark looked murderous, his face turning red with temper, and he asked, "May I call you?"

Kevin gave permission generously. "Sure."

But Lynn said, "Well, we're fighting a deadline, so we're really pretty busy."

"But you're not living together?" Mark glared at her.

"Yes," said Kevin.

"No," said Lynn.

And again the two looked at each other.

"Why fool him?" Kevin asked reasonably. "Your parents I can almost understand, but Mark is an old friend and open-minded."

Mark exhaled a blast like a bull seeing red, and Lynn became alarmed. Kevin was asking for it, but if they got physical they could knock over her plants, and anyway, Kevin might bleed and faint. She said to Mark, "Good luck on getting settled. I hope everything goes well for you." And she meant it.

"It's not," he replied sourly.

"Well, yes." She pretended to misunderstand. "You spoke of divorce, but maybe you can patch things up."

"No way."

"I'm sorry." Lynn was.

"It was a mistake from the beginning." Mark made that a meaningful sentence.

"That's too bad," Lynn sympathized.

"Lynn, I'll be in touch," Mark persevered. "We have a lot to talk about."

"No, actually, we don't," she disagreed. "And this deadline is really pushing us. We'll see you around, no doubt. Thanks for coming by."

But Mark was persistent. As he turned on the stairs he said again, "I'll call you."

Kevin leaned in the doorway and gave a loose hand wave, saying, "Anytime."

"Get lost!" Mark snapped.

"Not me!" Kevin grinned. "I know a good thing when I have it."

That was unforgiveable. Lynn reached up the back of Kevin's sweater and pinched his back. He gave a little jolt and growled low, but loud enough for Mark to hear, "Wait till he's gone, you wild woman!"

She gasped and turned to Kevin, and the door at the bottom of the stairwell slammed shut. "Now you can explain yourself!" she said. She made a stern face.

He looked very interested and asked, "What? What do you want me to explain?"

"Just why you deliberately made him think you were living here."

"Did I do that?" He appeared amazed.

"You know exactly what you did."

"Man, he really got mad, didn't he?" Kevin made a wonderful rumble of restrained amusement. "And he couldn't show it! He was in such a stranglehold, I really thought he'd burst a blood vessel! And then your current lover would have been forced to save the life of the castoff!" He laughed a rollicking, wicked laugh, very masculine and very pleased.

"But he thinks we're living together!" Lynn protested.

Kevin was expansive. "I'm perfectly willing to live here and save your reputation."

"'Save my reputation'? You've just ruined it!"

"Oh, that one. I meant your reputation for honesty," he elaborated. "If he and your nephew get it around that we're living together and people find out we're only sleeping together, your reputation for truthfulness is shot to hell. I'll move in," he assured her kindly.

"What if I wanted to be president?" she asked.

"Of what?"

"The country. These United States."

"Why would you want to do that? It's a terrible job!"

"What if the country needed me in a sensitive place and investigated me—" she waved her arms.

"I'd like to investigate your sensitive places," he confided, his voice a low, sexy rumble.

"And they uncovered this scandal about living with you?" she finished her sentence.

"It'd probably blow the investigation." He nodded sagely.

"You baffle me. I don't understand you." But her voice was very tender.

He came to her and took her into his arms, pulling her close. Very seriously he said, "Yes, you do, too, understand me. And you know exactly why I acted that way. Admit it."

"Admit what?" She lifted her face for his convenience, making her mouth handy. He was like no other man. He was uniquely himself, and she truly loved him.

"You even told him, 'We'll see you around.' That's what sunk him. You didn't say, 'I'll see you around.' You said 'we.'" He led her to that abominable sofa, and they sank down on it.

"I had to say it that way," Lynn told him. "If I'd

said 'I' he'd have thought I was interested in taking up with him again."

"And you're not." He made it a statement.

"No." She shook her head.

"And that's why I acted as I did," he explained. "I wanted it killed off right at the beginning. I didn't want him hanging around and confusing you."

"He couldn't confuse me," she admitted in a soft voice.

"He couldn't?" Kevin asked, encouraging her to elaborate.

"No." She ran her hands up his arms and cupped his head before she kissed his lower lip.

In a very low voice he asked, "Why couldn't he confuse you?"

"Because—" she sighed in surrender "—I love you madly."

"I knew that." He was smug.

"Did you?"

He nodded. "Did you know Ed sent me here deliberately? He and Ann talked about you. Ed's a dyed-in-the-wool romantic. And when you opened the door that first time, I knew we'd both met our fate."

"Why didn't you tell me?"

"When I came here I found a cringing woman, afraid of a relationship, expecting another rejection."

"I was not!" she disagreed. "I'll have you know—"

He went on as if she hadn't spoken. "Now you're an alive vibrant woman, facing the world on your own two feet. You're magnificent."

"So are you," she told him softly.

"It took you long enough to realize that."

"Every time I told you to leave and not come back, that I didn't want to get involved...."

"Ah," he said, "but it wasn't your words I listened to. It was how you kissed."

They kissed. His hands smoothed her shirt along her back with hard, petting strokes. He shifted her around, across his chest, and nuzzled her throat. He had to ask. "What did you think when you saw Mark again? Were you tempted?"

"No." It was the crisp casual word of indifference.

"He was clear he wanted to take up with you again. It's lucky for him I didn't knock him along the floor and out the front window. That would have been beautiful in slow motion." He paused, obviously savoring the mental image of Mark sliding slowly head first across the floor and out throught the front window.

"I'm glad you didn't." She arranged his hair into curls.

"Why? I might have marred that perfect profile?"

She mussed up the curls and replied, "You might have hurt your clever hands and bled...and fainted."

"My own blood and my own illnesses don't bother me. It's only someone else's."

"I love you, Terrance." She used his real name.

That deserved another kiss. Then he had to probe. "You weren't tempted at all?"

She thought of Kevin's superb act while Mark was there, and she smiled and touched his face with great loving tenderness. "You were outrageous, pretending you lived here."

"That was well-done, wasn't it." He grinned.

"That's because you're the writer. You instantly thought that charade up and acted it out perfectly."

"Without a rewrite!" he bragged.

She grinned at him and agreed. Then she said carefully, "My family would like to meet you on Saturday." Would like? They had set an ultimatum for the coming Saturday—a family dinner. Would Kevin survive, she wondered. Then she knew instantly that he would, with great aplomb.

"Why do they want to meet me?" Kevin asked. And his eyes glinted.

"Well, you see, I told them...I mentioned that we've been seeing each other a little...."

He reared up and loosened his arms and looked at her. "'A little'?" He seemed surprised. "There's more?"

"We're still living apart," she reminded him.

"That's a mere technicality. We'll solve that. I'd suggest we just go get married on Friday and arrive on Saturday at your folks' house with the fact. This would eliminate the shotgun jammed up my back."

"My father is more subtle than that."

"Will you marry me?"

She looked at him a little scared.

"Three's a lucky number," he assured her as he tightened his arms. Then he kissed her mouth in a lovely, cherishing way. He said huskily against her throat, "I'll make a deal with you—you have our babies, and I'll keep the house clean and cook."

"You promise?"

He nodded solemnly. "Total commitment."

"Good." Then she straightened up and called, "Did you get that on tape?" She pretended to hear an affirmative reply and yelled, "Okay. Wrap it up. Thanks." She settled back down and grinned at him. "It's a deal."

"Trapped," he complained insincerely. He kissed her again and massaged her various muscles, touching and kneading and exciting her. "I think you ought to make love to me," he said.

"Why ever would I do something as rash as that?" She kissed along his chin.

His arms tightened and his voice went low and husky again. "Because this is probably the first time you've realized that I am the only man you could ever really love."

It was true, and she told him softly, "I realize now I've known that all along. I just resisted."

"I find resistance annoying," he informed her. "Stimulating," he admitted, "but hampering."

"Who's resisting now?" She moved her shoulders in an enticing way so that her body moved in his arms, and she slid against him, making him suck in air through his teeth.

His eyelashes closed like a lion purring, and she possessed that erotic lower lip—as he worked his Martian magic on her.

HARLEQUIN
PREMIERE AUTHOR EDITION

6 EXCITING HARLEQUIN AUTHOR
—6 OF THEIR BEST BOOK

Daphne Clair
A STREAK OF GOLD

Marjorie Lewty
TO CATCH A BUTTERFLY

Anne Mather
SCORPIONS' DANCE

Jessica Steele
SPRING GIRL

Margaret Way
THE WILD SWAN

Violet Winspear
DESIRE HAS NO MERCY

Harlequin is pleased to offer these six very special titles, out of print since 1980. These authors have published over 250 titles between them. Popular demand required that we reissue each these exciting romances in new beautifully designed covers.

Available in April wherever paperback books are sold, or through Harlequin Reader Service. Simply send your name, address and zip or postal code, with a check or money order for $2.50 for each copy ordered (includes 75¢ for postage and handling) payable to Harlequin Reader Service, to:

Harlequin Reader Service

In the U.S.
P.O. Box 52040
Phoenix, AZ 85072-2040

In Canada
P.O. Box 2800
Postal Station A
5170 Yonge Street
Willowdale, Ontario
M2N 6J3

EYE OF THE STORM

MAURA SEGER

A powerful portrayal of the events of World War II in the Pacific, *Eye of the Storm* is a riveting story of how love triumphs over hatred. In this, the first of a three book chronicle, Army nurse Maggie Lawrence meets Marine Sgt. Anthony Gargano. Despite military regulations against fraternization, they resolve to face together whatever lies ahead…. Also known by her fans as Laurel Winslow, Sara Jennings, Anne MacNeil and Jenny Bates, Maura Seger, author of this searing novel, was named by ROMANTIC TIMES as 1984's Most Versatile Romance Author.

At your favorite bookstore in March.

EYE-B-1

Share the joys and sorrows of real-life love with
Harlequin American Romance!

GET THIS BOOK FREE as your introduction to Harlequin American Romance – an exciting series of romance novels written especially for the American woman of today.

Mail to:
Harlequin Reader Service

In the U.S.
2504 West Southern Ave.
Tempe, AZ 85282

In Canada
P.O. Box 2800, Postal Station A
5170 Yonge St., Willowdale, Ont. M2N 5T5

YES! I want to be one of the first to discover **Harlequin American Romance.** Send me FREE and without obligation *Twice in a Lifetime.* If you do not hear from me after I have examined my FREE book, please send me the 4 new **Harlequin American Romances** each month as soon as they come off the presses. I understand that I will be billed only $2.25 for each book (total $9.00). There are no shipping or handling charges. There is no minimum number of books that I have to purchase. In fact, I may cancel this arrangement at any time. *Twice in a Lifetime* is mine to keep as a FREE gift, even if I do not buy any additional books.

Name _____ (please print)

Address _____ Apt. no. _____

City _____ State/Prov. _____ Zip/Postal Code _____

Signature (If under 18, parent or guardian must sign.)

This offer is limited to one order per household and not valid to current Harlequin American Romance subscribers. We reserve the right to exercise discretion in granting membership. If price changes are necessary, you will be notified.

AMR-SUB-1

154-BPA-NAZJ